THE NOVICE

Timothy Ireland was born in Southborough, Kent in 1959. Since leaving King Alfred's College, Winchester with a degree in English and Drama, he has endeavoured to combine periods of full-time employment with having time to write. His previous publications include two novels for teenagers, *Catherine Loves* (1980) and *To Be Looked For* (1981).

Between 1982 and 1985 he lived in London. His third novel *Who Lies Inside* was published by GMP, earned considerable praise, and won the Other Award for 1984.

Presently, the author lives in Brighton, Sussex.

TIMOTHY IRELAND
THE NOVICE

First published in November 1988 by GMP Publishers Ltd
P O Box 247, London N17 9QR, England
Second impression July 1989

Distributed in North America by Alyson Publications Inc.,
40 Plympton St, Boston, MA 02118.

British Library Cataloguing in Publication Data

Ireland, Timothy, 1959-
        The Novice.
        I. Title
        823'.914

ISBN 0-85445-089-2

Printed and bound in the European Community
by Nørhaven A/S, Viborg, Denmark

Author's Note

All novels are rooted in feeling, and there is always some relation between the author and the characters he or she creates. Nevertheless, whilst this borrows some detail from my past, it remains a work of fiction and all of its characters are imaginary.

1

HE STOOD in the crowded bar just ten yards away from me. Maybe in his late twenties, a few years older than I was. Two heavily made-up girls, barely eighteen, eyed him from the nearest table. Arranging long arms and legs, calmly adult with glasses of Pernod and blackcurrant and cigarettes, they tried to catch his attention.

The man we were watching so closely wore blue jeans, a grey patterned shirt and an open black leather jacket. Slim and short and dark-haired, his wide-set brown eyes made his face striking. He stood straight-backed: one hand held his pint glass of beer, while the other rested deliberately on the broad steel buckle of his leather belt.

He switched his gaze round the bar, taking care not to rest his eyes on anyone, but I knew he was waiting. I knew because I too had stood like that amongst a crowd a hundred times.

He drove me to the tree-lined common in a battered Mini. I knew where to ask him to stop: just in front of the flaking wooden post that pointed the way of the winding public footpath through the wood. I'd lied and told him I lived ten minutes walk away. At this time of night I knew it would be quiet here. Less chance of being disturbed.

When the engine died I made no move to get out of the car; instead I concentrated on the sound of his uneven breathing. Staring out at the darkness, I licked my lips nervously. Anyone else would have thanked him for the lift and left.

There was a reason why I stayed in the car: and a reason why he'd offered me the drive home. The reasons balanced themselves, bought a shallow understanding. But we did not speak.

Slowly, his hand crept to my knee. As I tentatively reached down, he grasped my fingers tightly, still afraid to face me. The excitement flickered between us like heat, burned any words away.

As I turned towards him he gripped the back of my neck, pulling me closer and forcing his mouth against mine. Then, as if ashamed of his kiss, he twisted away. Hiding his face against my chest, he wrapped his arms tightly around me. I realised I didn't even know his name.

We stayed locked together for a long, awkward moment. Then, sliding sidewards against me, he tugged my arm towards his waist, put my fingers against his erection. A shudder went through us; at the same time I wanted to pull away from him. It was all happening too fast.

"Unzip."

Uncertain, still I obeyed him, stiffening as his fingers freed me from the tangle of cotton. He lowered his head, sucking me for a few startling seconds.

There was the moan of a car engine: a sweep of headlights exposed us and swept on. Jerking away from me, I could almost smell the fear seeping out of him. His lips trembled.

"Are we going to do it?" He swallowed half-way through the sentence.

Suddenly I was scared. Turning towards him, I wished he would only turn and look into my eyes. "Let's see each other again."

"Why? No point."

I realised that anything which happened now had to appear insubstantial, so it could be forgotten tomorrow and put aside. In wanting more I had disappointed him.

"I'll go then."

The car-keys jingled in his hand. He was going to drive away.

"Why not next week? Next Saturday: I could meet you in the same place."

"Next Saturday," he said, "I'll be watching *Dynasty* or *The Paul Daniels Magic Show*. Whatever's on TV. I'll be sitting in the flat with my girl friend. She's visiting friends this weekend. That's why I was in the pub."

"We could always meet in the week. Tuesday, say."

"*No.*"

Fumbling with the car door I found the handle-lock, pushed the door open and clambered out. As I stumbled across the grass without looking back, I heard the complaint of the engine as the car pulled away.

In retrospect, I recall it as a secret, something I'd kept from everyone, being a virgin still at twenty-three. Of course, I'd mucked around with girls, but actual penetration, what we used to call the Real Thing, was beyond my experience.

I'd had my chances in the sticky dimness of the disco-theque or on the dark walks back from the pub where we experimented, exchanging purple love bites like tattoos. I'd nipped and kissed and caressed several girls until the Time was Right. But on each occasion it had ended with me aware of their waiting for the next move, the puzzlement in their eyes when I drew away and straightened my clothes.

One girl had hungrily sucked me until I was hard. And another, trembling and uncertain, had peeled off her pants, looking at me wide-eyed across her narow bedroom one Sunday afternoon. I never felt disgusted or revulsed. There was just that complete absence of deep feeling, as though none of this had anything to do with me.

I didn't realise who I was then. Perhaps I was too romantic. I thought the girls I'd had chances with weren't the right girls. The time would be right when love was there, when the intimacy with another was making love, not *screwing* or *fucking* or any of the words used.

Sex without love, I reckoned, would be just like solitary masturbation; quick, barely satisfactory and, so soon afterwards, desolate and rather sad. So I waited for love, waiting as though for something that would never come.

In a sense, I settled for being no one. It was easier to do than you might think, living at home in a small world, cushioned by Mum and Dad. I didn't go out much. I stayed in and read in my bedroom, or listened to tapes or watched television on my black and white portable. The few friends I had said I was Quiet. If I got drunk and silly they called me a Laugh. Most of them were in boy-girl couples: married, engaged or living together. They had less and less time for me.

So I waited and waited for something to happen. Sitting like some frustrated hen trying to hatch a future. The young man who drove me to the common that night was the first man I'd ever kissed. For nights afterwards that kiss haunted me. I'd lie awake willing my body to recall every touch, playing back the furtive scenario with a hundred different endings.

I went back to the same pub the following Saturday, hoping. But he wasn't there. Still I'm grateful to him, whoever he was. Even if he went running back to his girlfriend, he'd brought about a beginning in me. Maybe not the one other people might have wished, but a beginning nonetheless. One that was right for me.

I remember now, it was less than a month later I bought my first copy of *Time Out* from the high street newsagent. The Lonely Hearts column in the back pages fascinated me.

GAY GRADUATE, 20s, slim, attractive, seeks genuine, caring friend 21-31, who likes theatre, music, good wine and being happy.

PROFESSIONAL GAY GUY, 42, Non-camp, ex-Royal Navy, seeks young muscular friend for evenings out, possibly more.

LONELY GAY MAN, attractive 33, solvent, own home, own car, seeks that someone special to share life with. Must be 21-35, slim, masculine, clean-shaven non-smoker who likes classical music, the outdoors and sharing Sunday newspapers in bed.

I wondered who these people really were; what sort of lives they lived; what jobs they did; what they looked like. Perhaps I would be the person one of these lonely men was looking for...

Of course, such an idea was absurdly romantic, but from childhood on I had spent countless Sunday afternoons lapping up the black and white melodramas repeated on television. I believed in the myths of films like *Now, Voyager* and *Casablanca*, and thought that somewhere out there my love awaited me.

It was as I studied the listings in *Time Out* that suddenly I felt sure that it was to London I had to go to find him.

"I saw your advertisement," I said from a phone-booth on Waterloo station.

"Sorry?" The voice was a mixture of irritation and vagueness.

"The advert for a room. Could I come and see it, please?"

"Oh yes. Yes, of course." By degrees his voice became more friendly as he gave directions to his Victoria flat.

"You can't miss it," he said at last, a swelling tone apparent down the crackling line. "I'm on the third floor. You can see the billboard of the Apollo Theatre from my sitting room window."

After this revelation, my possible landlord, Simon West, hung up.

Less than an hour later, I stood tentatively on the stone steps outside the Victorian mansion block and checked my wristwatch. Looking down the road, the theatre billboard (indeed in view) proclaimed, after many years and many marriages, the latest return of a former Hollywood starlet to the London stage.

In front of me, the push-button entryphone system was a source of puzzlement. Being a small-town boy I was unused to calling on anyone who didn't live in a house with a straightforward doorknocker or doorbell. Uncertain how to make my presence known, I kept my finger depressed on the push-button for a full minute.

Disembodied, a voice crackled out of the grill.

"Do stop that ringing!"

Embarrassed, I stood there frozen whilst the amplified sound of a dog barking drowned out the thin voice. Then the door buzzed and there was the click of the lock. Taking a breath, I pushed the heavy door open and stepped inside.

The entrance hallway was unwelcoming grey stone. A curious black snake-like pattern wound its way across the ancient tiled floor. Although it was early afternoon the main hallway was windowless and steeped in gloom. A curved staircase with a tarnished brass handrail led the way to the upper floors. At the foot of the stone steps was a dog, perhaps half alsation.

Despite being nearly six foot tall dogs had always made me nervous. As a paperboy I'd tremblingly slipped a newspaper through a glass door only to see the pane shake under the assault of a full grown collie. That memory lingered. Now, as I took a hesitant step forward, the dog in front of me barked, then sat back on its haunches, its long tongue lolling pink through white teeth. I've got this bugger on the run, it was thinking doggishly. Afraid to move, I started as a voice called down impatiently.

"Follow Bruno up the stairs."

Bruno wagged his tail, then turning on four paws, loped up the stone steps. Trailing behind, I felt I was the fly skittering towards the spider.

The lighting seenmed even dimmer on the third floor. A figure appeared abruptly in the doorway at the end of the narrow passageway.

"Mr West?"

The tall man nodded.

"I'm Donovan Crowther. I've come about the room."

Walking forward, I realised that Mr West was wearing a quarter-length black cape secured at the throat by a jewelled brooch. His neat-featured face was heavily lined and curiously empty of expression. He might have been seventy.

"Come in," he said, "And close the door behind you."

As I entered the wide hallway, I jumped at the sight of a face wracked with pain hanging from the ceiling. Then I realised that the whole hallway was filled with tormented heads. The smallest, set on shelves at eye-level, were no bigger than clenched fists. One or two were as tall as armchairs, but the most disturbing, suspended on wires from the ceiling, were human size.

At the end of the hallway, Mr West stretched out a thin hand to light a candle.

"You like the heads?"

"Well ..."

"A friend of mine sculptured them. They have a certain vitality, don't you think?"

"They look in pain. All of them."

Mr West looked pleased with this answer. He cleared his throat, eyeing me carefully.

"Of course," he said, "You're too young to understand that pain can be invigorating. Poor Daniel – whose work these heads are – can't feel anything now. A stroke, quite unexpected. If he gets better, if he's able to regain a little movement, his sisters will be able to look after him. They've wanted to get their hands on him for years."

"Why candles?" I interrupted.

Mr West licked his lips.

"They create atmosphere. They also save electricity."

He bustled through a doorway. At a loss I followed him.

In the sitting room there were also candles flickering in two brass candelabra perched on top of a piano covered with a green cloth. Though it was still afternoon, thick scarlet curtains had been pulled three-quarters of the way across the windows that would have revealed the sights of the town (and the billboard of the Apollo Theatre). The sound of traffic was muted, but almost deafening was the rhythmic *ticking*.

There were clocks everywhere; on the piano, the mahogany bureau, the writing-desk, the marbled mantelpiece and the small useless tables that cluttered the room. Some of the clocks were set in dark wood, some in brass or silver; others in bright art deco or pale carved ivory.

"The room," I managed at last, forcing the words out.

Prompted, Simon West leant back on the settee, stretching out an arm to a sidetable to stroke a green china crocodile with a clock-dial set in its pale belly.

"Simon West is my stage name," he began. "I am really Mr Wrigley." He smiled again, leaning forward into a full arc of candlelight to reveal his neat brown hair as a wig. Unaware, he bared his teeth. "But you may call me Simon."

I nodded.

"Your room," he said, rocking forward onto his feet and taking three tiny ballerina steps across the floor. "Follow me."

The tiny bedroom reminded me more than anything of a box at an old fashioned theatre. The walls were painted red, with gilded skirting board and picture rail. A raised narrow bed was covered by a smooth black coverlet with a glittering gold and green serpent stitched into it. Even the old mahogany wardrobe was hooded with thick scarlet drapes piped with gold brocade. The small oval mirror on the wall was fringed by cherry curtains tied with silver bows.

"Of course it is small," said Simon. "But very comfortable. Such a cheerful room I think."

"Very nice."

Simon sat heavily down on the narrow bed, his face unmoved by the creak of bedsprings.

"I think, Donovan," he said, chilling me with his use of my name, "I think you would like it here."

In the end it was just three days before I was due to transfer as a Clerical Officer from the Andover DHSS office to the Hammersmith office in West London, that I at last found a suitable bed-sitting room. My new home would be in Highlever Road, which in the London A-Z is somewhere between Ladbroke Grove and White City.

Although I had in part dreaded the disruption of leaving home, I think my parents were actually relieved to see me go. Not that they didn't love me, it's just that after twenty-three years of being responsible, caring parents they were quite pleased to know that from now on I would be looking after myself. The fact that I had previously survived three years away at college helped reassure them that I would be able to cope on my own.

On the eve of my departure from home, Dad took me out for a drink in the local pub. Mum declined to accompany us. I supposed her deliberate absence was to enable father and son to share a last moment of closeness. As I entered the pub behind my father, heard the music from the juke-box and the jangle of two fruit-machines, I wondered what there was we could say to draw us any nearer to one another in this time of goodbye.

"I've only been to London four times in my life," Dad said, thoughtful as a curate behind his pint of beer. "I never liked the place. Too many people."

"I'll get used to it." I wished I could have told him that it was the thought of all those people, all those different lives, that was drawing me to the capital.

"Of course, you're young enough to mix."Dad pondered. "There's a lot going on there. Theatres. Art Galleries. Museums ..."

Uncertain how to carry on, Dad stopped mid-sentence and took a draught of his beer. Even after twenty-three years we didn't really understand each other very well.

"If you don't get on in London, come home," Dad said.

"I will."

To mark my departure, my father ended the evening by ordering us both a whisky. He drank his straight down. I followed suit, anxious that I might choke and splutter and shame him, be something less than a man.

"The best then," Dad said. "The best."

At the train-station Dad held back hands in pockets. Mum, for some reason dressed in her best beige coat, came forward and took my arm, forcing a smile.

"It's not the end." she said. "You'll be home soon to visit."

I nodded to comfort her. But there was something final here. I felt just as I had when I left college, that a period of my life was over. Nothing would ever be quite the same.

2

MY LANDLADY, Mrs Milosevic, sat back in the wide blue armchair with Louis' head heavy in her lap. Louis, a large black chow, closed his golden eyes and allowed his ears to be scratched by his mistress's scented hands.

Perched shyly on the edge of the twin embroidered armchair, I was scared I would spill sherry on the deep-pile blue carpet littered with gold stars. The walls about me, also blue, were covered by paintings in heavy wood or gilded frames. Above a marble mantelpiece crowded with fine ornaments – figures playing musical instruments – was a tall mirror that reached almost to the white ceiling. It was the sort of room that feels a hundred years old.

"Welcome," said Mrs Milosevic, with a trace of accent. She raised her crystal sherry glass. "To both our healths."

I sipped my sherry self-consciously.

Mrs Milosevic parted pink lips, revealing neat white teeth that were probably false.

"You should have everything in your own room. If you have an unhappiness, let me know and we will have a chat."

I nodded on cue and, smiling, she carried on: "Visitors are your own affair. I do not worry what goes on behind the door as long as it does not disturb me. There is really only one rule. That is one of peace."

Mrs Milosevic ended her little speech with a gracious nod.

"I hope you will be happy here."

"Thank you." I downed the rest of my sherry anxiously

and had to muffle a cough behind my hands.

"I think you will want to settle in now."

Turning her face away dismissively, Mrs Milosevic put her hands, palm down, on top of Louis's head. The picture she made, reflected in the tall mirror on the wall, was naturally one of peace.

My room with apple-white walls bare of any pictures was simply, but for me, richly furnished. The wardrobe and giant chest of drawers were made of a dark wood that seemed to glow warmly. On one side of the window overlooking a garden was a stainless steel sink-unit with cupboards, a gas cooker and a small white refrigerator. A fold-up wooden table and two hard wooden chairs were in the middle of the room. A three-quarter bed – large enough for intimacy but too narrow to encourage a resident couple – was close against a wall with a gas-fire and a green cushioned armchair to one side.

To me it was perfect.

It was only later in the evening, after I'd heated and eaten my oven-ready chicken pie and oven-ready chips, that I felt lonely. There was no one to talk or idle with. No Mum smiling as she gave me a cup of tea. No Dad sitting rustling the newspaper. Even the chatter of the television was missing. I began to learn then what everyone who lives alone has to come to accept, that at the end of the day you have only four walls and your possessions for company.

I had never been to a gay pub before. As I walked the last few paces to the door, I couldn't stop myself glancing nervously down the street, wondering if any of the evening pedestrians would recognise me. What would they be thinking? The young man from the DHSS office a poof.

I suppose as I stepped inside the pub I'd expected the men to be all limp-wristed and effeminate like the caricatures in television comedies. But the men there looked just like the man in the street, the man who works in the office or comes to fix the plumbing. Many had moustaches or close-clipped beards but their ordinariness and their masculinity surprised me. As I made my way to the bar several men turned and looked, looked away.

Nervous, my face set in solemn lines. I wanted to smile, but couldn't.

I realised that despite the glances no one had smiled at me, there had been no trace of welcome. Trying to look cool, I asked for a pint of lager from a barman with cropped red hair and ripped jeans. As he moved away from the bar I saw the fleshy curve of one buttock exposed through a strategically placed tear.

Sipping my lager, I tried to relax. I was gay, this was a gay place, but that first first time I didn't feel at all at home. Hardly anyone was speaking. The majority of men were standing on their own, assuming deliberate poses of frozen nonchalance. I felt like a mannequin in a shop window. But was I attractive enough for anyone to talk to me?

Just before last orders someone shoved my shoulder from behind. I turned, uncertainly, to find a short stocky man in his forties looking up into my eyes.

"I've been watching you."

"Oh."

I was aware of his too tight jeans, the black leather jacket.

"Do you want to fuck?"

I just stood there.

"You'd look better if you smiled."

I nodded, scarcely able to breathe.

"I'm going," he said. "You coming with me? Worth your while."

The grey-haired man looked straight at me, the invitation like a challenge in his blue eyes.

"No thank you."

I turned back to the bar, my face set. I'd never thought it would be like this.

Although I told myself I would never enter the gay pub again, I knew nowhere else I could meet other gay people. And after all, we were all looking for something, someone. *There was always a chance ...*

The second time I went to the pub no one spoke to me. The third and fourth time was the same. My dread of the bluntest of propositions turned into corrosive self-doubt. Was something wrong with me? Foolishly, I questioned the mirror. Was I so unattractive?

Then one evening as I stood in the pub nursing my pint, I became aware I was being watched by a man at the end of the bar. He was in his thirties, heavily tanned with bleached blond hair.

As he looked into my eyes I felt the blood run to my face; an awkward charged feeling as if a line between the two of us had been suddenly drawn taught. We looked again. Eye to eye, but afraid to smile.

His neat brown moustache suited him. His dark-gold tee-shirt showed off his tan.

We looked again.

I tried to meet his steady gaze. It was as if I was holding a match, the flame flaring towards my fingers, burning. Glancing away, I kept my eyes averted and waited. Aware of the movement in the crowded bar, I could almost feel him come and stand beside me.

"Want a beer?"

Too nervous to trust my voice I nodded and he smiled for the first time. His name was Derek and he worked for a travel agent. We talked for ten minutes, uncertain of what words were right. He glanced at his watch twice. It was getting late, I suppose. And if I was going to let him down, there was little time left to find someone else. Perhaps he saw the doubt in my face, heard the reluctance creeping into my voice. Testing me, he put a strong hand on the square buckle of my belt.

"I like you."

I nodded, wanting to pull away, more certain I didn't want him. He let my belt go, tried another tack.

"There's a club down the road. Been there?"

"No.'

"It's a small club, but lively. Open till two."

Hesitating, I hid my face as I took a long draught of beer.

"Are you coming?" Derek suddenly sounded unconcerned.

Perhaps he didn't really want me. Perhaps he too was disappointed.

"Another time."

I meant No, never. We both knew that. And yet as he drifted away through the crowded bar, a part of me wanted to call him back.

One Friday night, a few weeks later, I ventured into the club on my own. It was tiny, about the size of two large living rooms and crowded with men trying to look their best in the thick atmosphere. There were two small bars, one at each end, both brightly lit and bustling. A swirl of colour from the miniature light-show accompanied the beat of the disco music. The DJ was playing a former disco hit, *It's Raining Men, Hallelujah!*. There was little space to dance, but two middle-aged men in jeans jiggled up and down, circling in a proprietorial way the thin figure of a rough-looking boy unsteady with drink.

It was as I turned back to the bar that I first saw him. As if aware of me, he looked up, finding me across the room. Our eyes met. Shyly, he dipped his chin and turned away. In his late thirties, he had short curly blond hair over the type of rugged face you'd imagine a farmer or a builder would have.

Slightly stern: only his eyes gave his gentleness away.

Looking at him, I was suddenly full of self-doubt. Precisely because I desired him, now I couldn't believe he would ever want me. Turning away, I tried to collect my thoughts and when I glanced back again he was pushing his way through the press of people, coming straight towards me.

Nervous, I avoided his gaze as he stepped by and made his way through the crush of people to stand at the other bar, less than six feet away from me. Trying to summon up the confidence to speak, I watched him buy a pint of lager, pocket the change then turn, glass to his lips, to look into my eyes.

Uncertain, I willed myself to take this chance. Slowly, I made my way to the bar. Standing close behind him, I took a breath and gave my order to the barman.

"Whisky, please."

At the sound of my voice, his head turned just a fraction. I could sense him tensing, waiting for the right moment. As I reached for my glass, he half turned to me, taking a quick look into my face.

"Shame they don't make whisky in Wales," he said.

We met each other's gaze, too nervous to smile.

"You're Welsh then?" I asked stupidly. His accent was strong, lilting.

"Blaengarw." He smiled. "Long while ago now."

"I'm new to London."

"Are you, now? It's a big place."

He hesitated then, thoughtful, and I saw for the first time the child in his face: a layer of innocence or simplicity, or neither of these things.

"You have a name then?' he said.

"Donovan Crowther."

"David Davies." He reached out a strong hand, that so close to me, shied away. "Mother named me after the Saint. Friends call me Davy."

We lapsed into faltering conversation. Then, interrupting

us, the barman called out "Time". Davy frowned.

"Thelights come on in a minute," he said. "Everyone is left looking at each other."

There was a pause. I wished I knew what to say.

"We've had a chat."

Uncertain, he reached out and took my left hand without looking at me.

"You a place, lad?"

Intent on silence, I shook my head, suddenly thinking of Mrs Milosevic and Louis watching me reprovingly.

"You see ..." Davy stumbled with his words. "There's people where I am, watching my business."

Saying nothing, I tightened my grip on his hand. A shiver ran between us. Davy reached down, grazed my arm with his fingertips.

"There is somewhere," he said at last, turning to me. "Will you come?"

Inside the expensively furnished basement flat, Davy's face became twisted with worry.

"You'd better take your shoes off if they're dirty."

"Davy ..."

I suppose I sounded frightened. He turned and came close to me. Strangers, we kissed awkwardly, lips nearly missing lips, apologetic almost.

"It's not my place," he said.

I swallowed. "It doesn't matter." I wished I could reassure him and by the reassurance somehow make this space ours.

"He's a terror for tidiness." Davy glanced apprehensively about the room. "When he gets back from holiday he'll be checking for dust."

The sense of dispossession made me shiver as if I'd heard footsteps in the hall.

Davy gestured to a framed portrait of a young man's face,

25

brown chalk on white paper.

"That's him there. When he was twenty-one."

I was afraid to look, but I couldn't help myself. The face, simply etched, seemed curiously inhuman. Perhaps my jealousy made it so.

"His folks are very well off. Flush." Davy indicated the ornamental china in a mahogany glass-fronted case. "He's a brainy fellow. Public school. And University."

The reverence in his voice unnerved me, and his words seemed to summon the stranger to whom the flat belonged, when I wanted no one but Davy and I to exist. Suddenly, I just wanted a place to hide.

"Where's the bathroom?"

"End of the hall. To your left." Davy gestured, bewildered. "Are you well?"

Hurrying along the hallway lined with glass-framed pictures, I found the door which opened onto an ivory bathroom suite. Shutting the door behind me, I took several deep breaths, trying to forestall the sudden sense of panic. Davy knocked on the bathroom door.

"Are you all right, boy?"

"Yes."

"Sure of it?"

I stole a breath.

"Davy ..."

I wished I could have told him that this was my first time with a man. I wanted him to *know*, but somehow know implicitly, without me putting anything into clumsy words.

Davy registered my hesitancy with concern.

"You sit there quietly a minute."

"Okay ..."

My voice trailed away. I wondered if everyone started out afraid of sex. I could feel the doubt cold inside me because no one had ever made love to me before. Could anyone actually want my body?

26

Afraid to look into the mirror, I tried to busy myself. After I'd had a pee and flushed the toilet, I found a toothbrush on a white bathroom rack and methodically cleaned my teeth. Then I washed myself with scented soap and hot water in the pedestal basin. Picking up a round green glass bottle, I dabbed some cologne on my face and wrists and sat quietly on the edge of the bath and waited.

Soon there was another knock.

"Better now?" Davy asked through the door.

"Yes."

"Coming out of your burrow then?"

Opening the door slowly, I stood reluctant, as Davy, now wearing a long white towelling dressing-gown, held out his hand. As I took it, he squeezed my fingers gently.

"Anything you'd like. Whisky'll settle your stomach."

I shook my head.

"I'd prefer tea."

"Nothing stronger?"

"Not for me."

Davy smiled. "Tea at two in the morning when all good folks are in bed."

Nodding, afraid to look at him, I hoped he understood. Slowly, Davy came and stood close to me. Stooping, I pressed my face against his throat, felt him swallow as I put my arms around him. His body was warm under the dressing-gown. For a long moment we stayed there not moving.

"You do want to stay?" Davy whispered.

"Yes."

Under Davy's touch my blood sang. His mouth, at times soft, at times biting, moved over my face and down my throat. His tongue circled my nipples, his hands exploring my back and thighs.

And then he stopped.

"There's some cream somewhere," he said, kneeling over me.

I turned my face away, intimidated by his experience.

"Haven't you ever been penetrated?"

"No." I could hardly breathe.

My nervousness wasn't because of the fear of AIDS. In those days the catastrophe was still to come. Not far away then, a shadow on the horizon, more than a whisper in America, but muted here, almost indiscernible. So it was not the fear of that disease which concerned me then, but the dread of the physical discomfort. Barely imaginable, I was only sure that such an act would hurt.

Davy gently considered my alarm. Looking down, he grazed my face with his fingertips.

"No matter," he murmured.

Afterwards we clung together in the dark, an awkward jumble of arms and legs, knees and elbows, trying to find a resting place. Before I had always slept alone. It was strange to lie there, preparing to sleep still wrapped in an embrace.

"Davy ..."

He put one finger to my lips.

"We'll have life stories another time."

But still I couldn't close my eyes.

"Can you remember my name?"

I turned my face up to him in the dark. Davy shifted closer and kissed me.

"Pleasant dreams, Donovan."

3

I DID not want to let him go. He lay, his face pressed against my neck, one broad arm flung across my chest, his body resting heavily against my side, breathing evenly in the peace that comes just before waking. While he slept my thoughts turned over. Still wondering at my feelings, listening to Davy's even breathing, I slipped into a shallow dawn-time dream.

Davy's voice woke me.

"Morning."

Blinking in the light, suddenly self-conscious, I sat up in the strange bed.

"I've made tea."

Sitting at the end of double bed, wrapped in the white towelling dressing-gown, Davy stole a glance at my face. Reaching forward, he passed me a mug of tea.

"Thanks." I took the proffered mug from him awkwardly. As I ventured to look into his eyes, we both smiled shyly, between us the memory of last night.

Now in the morning light, fierce through the half-drawn curtains, the lines on Davy's face were deeper. As he turned, I realised his fine curly blond hair was beginning to thin at the back. But I did not love him less. Rather, noticing these details etched him more clearly on my consciousness.

"Deep in thought, boy."

Nodding, I worried suddenly at what Davy might be noticing about me in the harsh light. Vulnerable, I hunched my shoulders, cradled the tea in my lap.

"When I got up you were sleeping as sound as a baby," Davy said. "Seemed a shame to disturb you."

Somehow by speaking he retreated from me. It had all felt so easy holding him while he was asleep. Now I realised how little we knew each other. Sitting up, I reached out and rested a hand on his arm, trying to find something to say.

"That dressing-gown fits you perfectly."

Davy shrugged.

"It should do. It's mine."

Unaware, Davy leaned forward and kissed me. *His* dressing-gown in a flat that belonged to the man in the chalk-portrait. The two of them, him and Davy, had almost certainly shared this bed. Turning my face away from him, I climbed out of bed and walked to the window, wishing I could escape, simply walk through the glass.

"Don ..."

Davy came up behind me, reached for my hand.

"What's wrong, boy?"

I wondered how many times he'd been in this situation before, how many other lovers there had been? I tried to find my voice.

"Can I have a bath ...?"

"Sure." Davy's puzzlement disappeared behind a smile. "I'll go run the water for you."

Whilst I bathed and dressed, Davy cooked us both a fried breakfast: bacon, eggs and mushrooms. After we'd eaten, I made coffee, Davy instructing me where the mugs and teaspoons were kept.

"What do you do for a living, Don?"

"I work in a Dole Office."

Davy raised his eyebrows.

"Busy, I expect."

"Most of the time. And pressured. My predecessor was beaten up."

"Your what?"

"Predecessor. The man I took over from."

Davy nodded approvingly. "You talk like a college boy."

"I studied Art History."

"Painting and that. Could you paint me?"

"I could try...I've mainly studied the history. Written essays rather than drawn."

"Fancy having a talent."

"I'm not special or anything."

"Course you are." Davy grinned. "I couldn't draw so much as a barn-door. Writing a note to the milkman's my limit when it comes to letters."

Ducking my head, I willed myself to ask: "Are you doing anything today?"

Davy frowned.

"I've made my plans."

Decisively, he stood up, collected both our plates together and put them in a plastic bowl in the kitchen sink, turned the hot water tap on.

"Tonight then?" I ventured.

"I'm busy tonight."

I watched Davy rinse the soapsuds off the knives and forks.

"I've a bit of tidying to do here." He glanced round at me quickly. "You be off and enjoy the sunshine."

I walked slowly into the sitting room to put on my shoes. On the mantelpiece beside a brass antique clock was a snapshot of Davy, bare-chested. Someone out of the photograph had flung a muscular arm round his shoulder. Davy was laughing.

In the silence I reeled round the room, clumsily searching for my keys and wallet.

"Besides the decanter," Davy said from the doorway.

"Will I see you again?"

There was a pause.

"At the club sometime. Soon." Davy dipped his chin.

Did he mean it? I wanted to kiss him to bring the closeness back, but I knew if I tried to he would move away.

"At the club, then." Suddenly I couldn't say his name.

For just a moment at the front doorway our faces were close, but almost involuntarily Davy backed away.

"Cheers, Don."

"Cheers."

As I turned, I heard him shut the door behind me. I almost ran up the basement steps. Opening the railing gate I hurried down the wide pavement, ignoring the looks of two builders on the other side of the road turning wet cement with a spade. Glancing at my watch, I saw that it was just after eleven. Already the sky, a pale summer blue, promised sunshine.

Later, in the confines of my bed-sitting room, my hands shook as I made myself a solitary cup of coffee. Sitting stiffly in the lone armchair my body ached for Davy. Drowning in silence, still I couldn't have suffered the chatter of the radio. I realised I couldn't even remember the name of the road or the number of the basement flat where only hours ago we'd been together.

I must have fallen asleep in the end. When I opened my eyes the room was in darkness. For a moment I hardly knew where I was. Surfacing, turning on a lamp, I looked at the alarm clock on my bedside table. It was quarter to eleven. I'd lost nearly seven hours. The pubs would be calling Time by now. Checking my hair in the mirror, suddenly everything was clear. I would go to the club where last night this change had begun. There, Davy would be waiting for me.

Back in the narrow room filled with men, I watched the eye to eye contact, the tilted cigarettes and soft exhaltation of blue smoke. Still in a dream, I nodded at the shy gleam of teeth, the glitter of a gold thread draped around a thin wrist.

It was so familiar from the night before, a sea of faces constantly turning in shivering courses.

There was no sign of Davy yet at the club. He would come later.

A man in his forties with thick grey hair, pushed past me in jeans and a leather jacket. He caught my eye and I remembered him from my first time in a gay pub – the man who'd asked me if I wanted a fuck.

Without registering my presence, he jostled through the tide of men and found a space against the wall. Slowly, he lit a cigarette, all the time glancing about him, up and down the club, waiting for a hesitation, the smallest sign of interest in another's eyes. Like the loneliest man in the world, he looked and looked and looked.

As I turned away from him, I recalled Davy saying he'd made plans for the day. Remembered the chalk portrait in the flat and the mantelpiece photograph of Davy bare-chested, laughing. Then my body summoned last night. The brown nub of Davy's nipples, the curve of his side.

I stood in the club waiting for him until closing time. But Davy never came.

In the old movies the Hollywood stars are able almost to turn back time, to mould the moments to ensure a Happy Ending. But every moment is finite: there is no going back, not to yesterday, not even to five minutes ago. Everything that has happened is sealed away out of reach.

Perhaps love connects the repetitive events and random incidents, gives us a sense of continuity and content. Davy now ran through every hour, threading my days together. In just three days his name had become my heart-beat. My pocket diary recalls my single-mindedness.

June 8: *No Davy.*

June 10: *Went to club in search again. No sign of him.*

On June 11 there is no entry. A complete blank, although I went to the club again and found Davy there.

He was standing against the far wall in jeans and a blue and white tee-shirt, holding a pint of lager. He nodded as he saw me uncertainly approach him.

"It's good to see you, Don.'

"I missed you."

He undid my shirt one button at a time. We took it in turns to remove each other's clothes, laughing at the moments of awkwardness; an arm caught in a shirt, a sock trapped tight on a heel.

The lightness of our feathered touches, whispers of mouth, fingers and tongue set us both falling. There was no urgency. No one-sided conquest. We took our pleasure evenly, swapping delight for delight.

"Have you ever penetrated a man?" Davy asked later, kneeling over me.

I shook my head, half-afraid of what he meant. Davy stroked my forehead softly.

"You can enter me. Don. I've some cream somewhere,"

He kissed me, touched my side.

"I'd like you inside me."

I swallowed.

"Won't it hurt?"

Davy smiled.

"Not me, lad. I've had the practice."

Later still, we lay together breathing deeply, wet in each other's arms.

"I thought I'd never see you again."

"Never?" Davy wiped the perspiration off his brow with the back of his hand. "Now never's a long time. A lot can happen between now and never."

"I went to the club three times and you weren't there."

34

Davy clumsily kissed my cheek, then lay back, resting his hand on the pillow. I held him tightly in my arms.

"I've been thinking about you, mind. Sooner or later, I said, I'll see that boy at the club. And there we are." He laughed and sat up on one arm. "You've had a man before. Expert you were."

"Never that way."

"First time lucky then."

"Davy...there's never been any man but you."

His silence expressed his surprise. Then he reached out, his fingertips grazing my face, his gaze intent before he grinned.

"Fancy me with a novice."

We kissed in the dark, settled back under the thin summer coverlet.

"Davy?"

"What now?"

"Tell me about yourself."

"My job you mean. I'm a chef of sorts. Nothing fancy, though I went to college, did my City and Guilds years ago. I'm in a cafe round Warren Street. I used to be in the merchant navy. I've travelled the world. Lisbon. Cape Town. Singapore."

"A boy in every port?"

"Some boys. Some women. Black as well as white. Perhaps I've even left kiddies behind me. I'd like to think I have somewhere a little Davy Davies running around."

"So why did you leave the navy?"

"I lost my sea-legs. Too many places. Too many trips. No home to call your own. No time to take up roots. You get tired of it." He shrugged. "I left three times. Had spells on shore working some place. Once on a farm, dipping sheep, shearing. Another time in a bar in Cardiff. The last time I left the sea I didn't go back. I shan't now neither."

"And Wales?"

"I was born in a small town round a mine. My Da worked

down the mines. It wasn't for me, not breathing coal dust in the dark, bent double, coming home smoky. The sea seemed clean ..."

Restless, Davy turned over in the dark, his back to me. Gently, I kissed both his shoulders, wondering at the man inside.

The next morning I sat in the garden at the back of the flat watching Davy watering a rainbowed border of flowers. Relaxed, he paused at intervals, admiring the sturdy delicacy of the blooms. His hands caressed the pink and yellow roses as tenderly as the heads of small children.

"They get thirsty," he said, over one shoulder. "All this sunshine dries them out."

I hesitated, always shy of questions with him.

"Do you have a garden of your own?"

Davy smiled to himself.

"Oh no, nothing so grand. A bedsit in the Harrow Road. There's a garden at home in Wales. Used to be my mother's pride and joy. Hours she spent there in the Spring. She worked hardest then so that she could enjoy the summer sitting out. No minute is wasted in a garden, Mam would say."

"Is your mother still in Wales?"

"Oh no. No. Mam died eleven years ago. Cancer. It's wicked. Mam never touched a cigarette in all her life."

Holding my breath I was afraid to say anything. Davy shook the last drops of water on the pansies, yellow and purple with black clown faces.

"Chattering away, I am." Davy slowly set down the watering can against the back wall. "Before we can go shopping, I've got the housework to do. Rob asked me to keep the flat tidy while he was away."

Rob. Now the man in the chalk portrait had a name.

Davy caught the dead look in my face and stepped towards me. Suddenly I couldn't help myself.

"When is he coming back?"

My voice stopped Davy only inches away from me.

"Tuesday," he said quietly.

For a long moment we couldn't even look at one another. I found myself clenching and unclenching my hands.

"I was meaning to tell you."

Davy's voice jarred in the uneasy quiet. I wanted to say everything was all right – that it didn't matter...But the words wouldn't come.

I pushed my way through the summery crowd in the street market in the Portobello Road, my mind racing. I suppose I'd believed that Love would make everything secure. But in three days time Rob would be back to reclaim his home. What was Rob to Davy...? There were so many questions I wanted to ask. Worse, I knew that none of them could be spoken now. Davy's sudden change of mood countenanced no enquiries.

Looking ahead of me I saw Davy striding on through streams of West Indians, Africans, Asians, Irishmen, and the tourist Japanese and Americans decked out in trendy shirts and sunglasses. Hurrying up the teeming road I caught up with him as he hesitated in front of an impatient taxi whose frowning driver sought a path through the tourists, the publishers, pedlars and punks. As I discreetly ran my hand up his bare arm, Davy gave me a quick look. Wanting to reassure him all I could think of was five words.

"It will be all right."

Davy nodded slowly.

"When we've done the shopping," he said, " we'll head out to the park."

In Kensington Gardens we lay on our bellies in the long

grass as close to one another as we dared.

"If I reach out I can touch you."

"Be my guest." Davy rolled over.

"You'll get me excited."

"Will I?"

We both grinned. The earlier tension brushed aside, I thought how I'd never felt so relaxed out in the open with another man. The person inside me, the homosexual no longer a stranger, embraced me as the sun reaching through the trees embraced my whole skin.

Maybe everything would be all right?

Closing my eyes, I sensed Davy move towards me. Leaning over me until I could feel his breathing, he tickled my face with a long strand of grass. Laughing I sat up quickly and we were as close as two lovers in bed.

At the same time, nearby a young woman pushed a baby in a pram along a winding path, accompanied by a young man holding the hand of a toddler in a bright cartoon tee-shirt. Davy rolled away from me, picking the grass self-consciously off his jeans.

"They weren't watching," I said.

"There's people all round us enjoying the sun. I was forgetting myself."

"We shouldn't have to be afraid of who we are."

"Easy to say, boy."

Davy turned his head to follow the progress of the couple with their young children.

"You should get yourself a wife and child," he said, "Before it's too late."

Stung, I tried to shrug off his words. Davy rose to his feet.

"We best be going now." He clapped his hands against his thighs.

"I was enjoying the sun."

"Can't lay around all day."

We exchanged glances, uncertain again. I wished I could

have stayed here under the trees forever. That life could be as simple as lying in the sunshine on a summer afternoon.

"Maybe there's time for a lunchtime drink," Davy said.

He began to wander away from me over the grass, then turned and stood still, waiting for me to catch up. As I walked into his shadow he looked right into my eyes, shy for a moment, but for once holding my gaze.

"I get my moods," he said. "I'll make it up later, in bed."

4

CANDLES FLICKERED on the yellow formica-topped table where dinner was laid out for me: a starter of prawns and avocado mixed with mayonnaise and seasoned with pepper, served in a whisky glass; beside it a white kleenex carefully folded into an upright hat-napkin.

"Davy ..."

He was watching me from across the narrow table, self-conscious, wanting me to be pleased.

"There's wine too," he said. "From the off-licence across the road. Liebfraumilch."

"It sounds grand."

"Sit you down, then."

Manoeuvering myself onto the small hard-backed chair, I banged a knee on one of the rickety table-legs.

Davy dipped his chin.

"No room to swing a cat."

"It's *fine*."

Nervous, I smiled, trying to reassure him. He'd been uncomfortable ever since I'd arrived at his bed-sitting room, a cramped square at the top of a tall, four-storeyed Victorian house just off the Harrow Road. Earlier, he'd told me to keep my voice down as the man in the adjacent room apparently eavesdropped. A Pole who worked for London Transport, he'd deliberately left the door of his room across the hallway slightly ajar. 'So he can peep out,' Davy said.

Now I watched Davy move to the small refrigerator in the

kitchen area of his room. Bending down, he took out the bottle of wine and searched for a corkscrew in a narrow cupboard drawer. A tape of the *Carpenter's Greatest Hits* played on his cassette-radio so we wouldn't be overheard. But even the soothing silky voice of Karen Carpenter couldn't melt the tension. It was the first time I'd seen Davy for nearly a week. Rob had returned to the garden flat days ago.

"We'll let the wine breathe." Davy put the tall bottle between us on the table. "Eat up your prawns."

"Where's yours?"

"I ate at work. It saves money. Tell me what you think of the avocado?"

Never an adventurer with food, I tried a spoonful and was pleasantly surprised.

"It's good."

"It's the high-life with me, lad."

We both smiled.

"Thank you, Davy."

"You've not but begun, lad." He smiled at me again. "Let's try the wine."

He poured my white wine into a whisky tumbler and, having no other glasses, he half-filled a purple and silver Aries star-sign mug for himself.

"It'll do," he said, after a taste.

His lilting Welsh voice moved inside me like a tongue, but it was Rob's name that reverberated inside my head.

Davy's surprise meal was chicken, fried first, then put into a thick mushroom and green pepper sauce. There were also roast potatoes, tomatoes, peas and sweet corn.

"It's a simple meal," Davy said, "But better for you than all those frozen pies you've been heating up."

"You sound like my mother."

Davy half-smiled, then hesitated, his face set.

"Do your parents know about you?"

The question so unexpected made me stop for breath. I looked down, embarrassed.

"I want to tell them," I said at last.

Davy watched me slowly pick up my knife and fork.

"Why cause them trouble?" he said.

"I want them to know. For me, it's important."

Davy hesitated, then put down his mug and rested his hands palm down on the narrow table, and I was aware he wanted to touch me. Then he shrugged, his thoughts still turning over.

"I wouldn't have the words to tell anyone, lad. Not a thing like that. Wouldn't know where to begin."

"But don't you feel you're hiding?"

Davy shook his head.

"It's not London everywhere, Don. In a small town in Wales a man hides things. He has to. I won't change now."

For some reason his words disquieted me. Perhaps the certainty in his voice exposed my inexperience. Made me feel I was dreaming. In that moment I wanted the truth; believing in truth there was security. Wiping the mushroom sauce from my mouth with the improvised paper-napkin, I tried to steady my voice before I spoke.

"Have you met Rob since he came back?"

Davy took a large swallow of wine.

"I went round for dinner with him."

"When?"

"Yesterday evening."

Yesterday ...So today it was my turn.

Standing up abruptly, I upset my whisky tumbler full of wine. Almost in slow motion the glass rolled off the table onto the floor, shattering.

"Damn ..."

I took a deep breath.

I knew he would never love me.

"*Donovan.*"

Kneeling on the floor beside the broken glass I hid my face. Davy stood over me. I could feel him there as if he cast a cold shadow on my back.

"Don...listen. I told him about you." Carefully, I picked up a bright shard of glass. 'He told me not to come back. Rob was always the jealous type."

I was still afraid to look up.

"Don, it's over and done with."

Was it?

Fucking is always so easy in books. Just the faintest trace of virginal blood and only for the first time pain. Was it really so simple?

That night, I let Davy manoeuvre me onto my back and explore me with his fingers and tongue. I watched him rise from the bed and search in the top of the chest of drawers for a tin of skin cream. Apprehensive, I saw himself cream himself and approach me.

"Can I enter you?"

I swallowed. "You know I've never done it before."

"This'll be your first time then. Just relax."

"I'm not sure I can."

He kissed my shoulder.

"I won't hurt you."

Lying back beneath him, I closed my eyes, wanting to give him what he wanted.

But it did hurt.

"You have to relax, that's all."

Davy applied more cream to both of us, pushed harder into me, and I started with the shooting pain.

"Don, you must relax."

"*I can't.*" There were tears of frustration in my voice. I pressed the side of my face into the pillow, wanting to hide as Davy stood up and left me. Returning moments later, he put a glass to my lips.

"Drink this."

"What is it?"

"Whisky."

I took several large swallows. It must have been at least four measures.

"Drink it all."

"You'll get me drunk."

Davy didn't smile.

"It will help you to relax."

Forcing the whisky down, I told myself I wanted this, I wanted this to happen. It was all a part of love.

The first time was not magic for either of us. There were no bright lights, no surge of blissful emotion. I didn't open up to Davy like a flower. After ten minutes painful prodding, Davy gave up.

"Do you hate me?" Davy asked, as we lay together sticky and frustrated.

"No ..."

But I was afraid of being taken that way, worried that my fear would spoil our love-making. Whenever we undressed now, whenever we kissed, there would be this expectation hanging over me. It was not simply the physical discomfort of penetration, but the dread that my resentment and Davy's disappointment would return the next time we tried and the time after that. Worst of all was a contaminating sense of failure.

Davy kissed one of my nipples, turned the caress into a biting action. As I started, he held my gaze, trying to smile. I could sense him struggling to understand my feelings, trying to reassure me, but he did not know how.

"It still feels sore." I was nervous.

He licked one of my nipples, kissed the other.

"I was only a little way in."

"I thought flesh would give way to flesh, but it was like a

knife."

"You were scared, that's why. If you relax then you loosen up. All it takes is practice."

Sighing, I couldn't meet his gaze.

"I think I want the toilet."

"Do you have to?"

"Yes."

"Poor mite."

Standing up, I was suddenly afraid that sitting on the toilet I would begin to bleed.

"Put your clothes on," Davy said. "You can't go downstairs naked."

Dressing in silence, I wished Davy could have come and hugged me, but he hung back. Watched me fumble with the latch on the door.

When I came back, Davy, wearing a blue cotton dressing-gown, was making coffee.

"How was it?"

"I farted Nivea."

Davy smiled, as I'd intended him to. But still he didn't come and comfort me. Uncertain, I sat down defensively in the room's only armchair.

"Coffee will help," Davy said.

Watching him pour hot water from the kettle into two mugs, I wondered if talking would make me feel better. My inexperience had made me curious.

"Davy...what was your first time like? When someone tried to get inside you?"

"Sore, boy. I was sore for days. I was older than you, mind. Still it hurt."

"Who was your lover?"

"A school-friend."

"School?'

"He'd left school by then, Don. Got married. When he took me it was at his house. We must have had a whole pot of cream. He wasn't as gentle as I was with you. His wife was sitting downstairs."

"*Downstairs?*"

My voice shook.

"Didn't his wife know what was going on?"

Davy shrugged, oblivious.

"Probably," he said. "Nothing was said then. But she doesn't mind his affairs. As long as he leaves other women alone. They've kids now. Look, see the picture there on top of the chest of drawers. That's me holding his youngest, Samantha. Four years old then."

Lost for words, I picked up the photograph, stared at it numb and confused. Through the glass the image of Davy looked up at me, smiling. On his knee sat a little girl in a blue dress, her long dark hair falling over her lacy white collar. She was pretty, her eyes fixed on Davy adoringly, one small hand reaching up to his face.

Five days later, Davy still hadn't rung me. In the end I made myself go out on my own to an evening showing of a film called *Heat and Dust*. Set in India at the time of the Raj, the film ends with the shamed English heroine exiled to a solitary house at the foot of the mountains where she wastes her life away waiting in vain for her older Indian lover.

As the credits rolled and the house lights of the cinema came up, I watched the couples in the audience shuffle out, reaching for another's arm, joining hands, exchanging a secret smile.

On the bus-ride home I sat near the front in one of the sideways benchseats. A young girl with cropped red hair and violent purple face make-up, sat opposite me dressed all in black. Despite her aggressive guise, her feet in buckled army boots barely reached the floor. The dark-skinned bus-conductor, middle-aged and used to far more bizarre sights, chatted to the punk girl quite amiably.

At the next stop a tall, burly man in a brown tee-shirt and dusty trousers staggered onto the bus. Unsteady with drink, the man fell back into the seat beside me as the bus accelerated sharply forwards. Red-haired, perhaps forty, the man joked loudly with the bus-conductor in a slurred Irish accent as he fumbled with his change, trying to pick the right coins out of his palm. Mopping his broad brow with the back of his hand, he turned and registered the girl sitting opposite him.

"Give us a smile, darling."

She turned her head away and defensively took a firmer hold on the bulging plastic bag in her lap.

"Come on, smile sweetheart."

He lurched forward, almost a comic picture, a hand cupped to one heavy red ear. The diminutive girl turned like a thorn to face him.

"Why don't you piss off ?"

Standing over her, the drunk took in her shapeless black shirt, the high-laced army boots and the broad silver studded belt. His thick lip curled.

"You're a butch girl, aren't you? Men not good enough for you?"

"Get lost."

"Lezzie. I know what you need."

He lurched closer. I could feel the girl's fear like a damp wall.

"What you need is cock, girlie. I've a mind to give it to you."

The girl tried to straighten her shoulders to face him.

"Screw yourself."

Swaying forward, the drunk struck the girl, sending her sprawling back in the seat. As he leaned over her, reaching out with his strong arms, she kicked at him, her thin legs flailing like a child's. And he struck her again.

I'd learned about Love from the movies. From the restraint of Celia Johnson and Trevor Howard in *Brief Encounter* to the realisation of Shirley MacLaine and Jack Lemmon in *The Apartment*, the romantic melodramas had captured me. In the movies romance never died. The modern film factories still churned out dreams. Against a Vietnam background, Jane Fonda and Jon Voight still found one another in *Coming Home*. Despite being married to other partners, in the closing frames of *Falling in Love*, Meryl Streep and Robert de Niro ended up safely in one another's arms.

In the florist's in Holland Park, I watched the middle-aged assistant carefully select a single stemmed rose from a host of others clustered in a tall green plastic vase. Catching my eye, she almost smiled at me, perhaps imagining the girl I was courting.

Silent, I let the woman put the rose and a spray of fern into a transparent plastic tube wrapped round with a lacey red ribbon. Such extravagant packaging made me shy. Perhaps the woman read my thoughts – or in her profession was sensitive to the self-consciousness of the romantic – because she wrapped the gaudy tube up in a thick sheet of brown paper, taking care not to crease the red ribbon.

It was raining, chill droplets beating into my face as I hurried down the road to Davy's bed-sit, the brown-paper covered tube tucked awkwardly under one arm.

Ringing the doorbell I waited until the heavy door was opened by a large lady in her fifties wearing a light-blue flowered dress.

"Is Mr Davies in?"

"Upstairs in his room." She looked at me without interest, took a step back into the hall. "Fearful change in the weather," she said. "These weathermen are born liars."

Shaking the rain off my coat, nervousness and anticipation crackled like electricity within me.

"I'll see my way upstairs."

The lady nodded, disappearing into a brightly-lit sitting room.

Creeping quietly up the stairs, I wondered what Davy's reaction would be to my surprise call. On the third floor the light was on in the bathroom on the landing, making me hurry up the last flight of stairs so I wouldn't be seen by any of his neighbouring tenants.

Music was coming from Davy's room. Straining to hear, I recognised the voices upraised in a neatly woven love song – Abba's *Fernando*. I was just a kid at school, twelve or so, when the record had first come out. Turning a corner in my memory, the florist's wrapping paper crackled under my arm as softly, holding my breath, I turned the handle and opened the door.

There was a man lying bare-chested in Davy's bed, a white sheet pulled up to his waist. I was aware of the thick black hair and olive skin, the neat moustache and the dark eyes alight with surprise.

"Davy...he's in the shower." The man gestured, not moving from the bed where less than a week ago I had lain.

5

MRS MILOSEVIC knocked on my door and called out my name as if summoning a small child.

Opening the door hesitantly, I felt curiously undressed in my red tee-shirt and blue shorts. But Mrs Milosevic, wearing a white cotton dress and a scarf of blue and purple flowers, was already retreating down the hallway with her large black chow, Louis, padding behind her.

"Donovan," she said clearly over her shoulder. "Come into the sitting room for a morning coffee."

It was Saturday, just after ten o'clock. Wondering at the unexpected invitation, like a schoolboy I expected some sort of disciplining. Mrs Milosevic wavered in the hallway like a white ghost, clearly expecting me to follow. Lifting her narrow bony shoulders, she sighed, flapping her hands like fans.

"It is so hot," she said. "I burn even with the windows open."

My shorts indirectly excused, I followed her down the stairs which she took slowly, one at a time, suddenly confined to an older person's gait. Louis padded patiently after her.

In the blue-walled sitting room I avoided my reflection in the tall mirror reaching almost to the ceiling. Between the gilded-framed pictures, curtains draped over open windows billowed in the slight breeze. A china flowered coffee-pot and matching cups, sugar bowl and milk jug, were laid out on a dark wood tray set squarely on a green padded footstool.

Mrs Milosevic settled herself in a huge armchair, arranging white cushions about her like pillows.

"Will you be mother?" she requested softly, her hands pulling a little at her scarf.

For no reason at all quite suddenly I wanted to cry. Davy had done this to me.

My hands trembled as I poured the coffee and added milk and sugar at her promptings. Averting my face I gave Mrs Milosevic her cup and saucer, afraid she might read my feelings in my eyes.

"I have some bad news," she said, apologetically, as I sat down.

Nodding, I felt absurdly certain she was going to throw me out because she didn't want a homosexual in her house.

"You've been such a good tenant," Mrs Milosevic went on, ruffling Louis' dark ears. "No noise, no parties and no visitors. We hardly ever see each other. Everything is perfect." She paused, waiting for my assent and I nodded, catching her liquid gaze for just a moment.

"Our agreement was for six months, wasn't it, Donovan?"

"Yes ..."

"Unfortunately," Mrs Milosevic declared, "my relations are coming to vist earlier than I had expected. They will be here in six weeks time."

"So you'd like me to go?"

"In six weeks time. Would that be acceptable to you?"

"Yes." At that moment I didn't care. Saw only the man lying in Davy's bed.

"You have time I think to find somewhere else. I will give you a reference if you wish. I am sorry for the muddle."

Mre Milosevic seemed to pause, one hand carefully adjusting her flowered scarf. Perhaps she was waiting for me to tell her it was all right, it didn't matter, it was fine. But all three phrases were tidy lies. We finished our coffee in silence.

"Such hot weather," Mrs Milosevic began, as I put my cup and saucer back on a tray.

Forcing a smile, I nodded.

"Thank you for the coffee."

Mrs Milosevic graciously declined her chin, and I was dismissed.

How could one human being ever belong to another?

So Davy told me, but I did not want to believe that such belonging was impossible, that Love could be anything other than complete.

At the other end of the telephone line Davy waited patiently. But still the words wouldn't come.

"Are you there, Don?"

Uncertain, but concerned, it was hard to believe from his voice that he could have hurt me.

"I can't talk now."

Aware of my work colleagues around me, sitting at their desks, shuffling through an endless pile of claim forms, I tried to soften my voice.

"You'll come round this evening, then?" Davy said.

How many times had the young moustached man been with him?

"No ..."

"Then meet me at Holland Park. Please, Don. I'll see you by the main entrance at six."

Davy was waiting for me with flowers; orange tiger-lilies and deep blue irises. He held them awkwardly, upside down like an umbrella. It hurt to smile at him. As I drew close, Davy put the flowers between us.

"For you."

Glad of something to distract me, I fixed my attention on the long-stemmed blooms.

"I don't know what to say, Don." He avoided my eyes.

I wished he would be silent; that silence could heal the rift between us. But at the same time I wanted words, a whole shower of them – to reassure, to explain, to console – to put everything back where it had been.

Davy moved to take my hand, then stopped, remembering this was a public place. Facing me, I was aware of his eyes darting self-consciously away from the flowers he'd given me.

"I was worried about you, lad."

Not knowing what to feel, I stared at the ground.

"I knew you'd take on so."

"Wouldn't you?" My voice was strained, yet my body ached for reconciliation, the flowers trembling in my hand.

"It wasn't what you thought," Davy said.

"You mean you didn't have sex with him?"

"I was in the shower."

"Was that before or afterwards?"

Davy ducked his head.

"If I thought you'd be like this, I wouldn't have come here," he said.

"Do you have any idea what I feel..?"

Davy's face twisted two ways.

"Let's stop these words, Don."

Turning my head, looking back along the elegant street, I lost my gaze amongst the heavy branches of the green, pedestrian trees.

"I've money for a meal," Davy ventured. "I thought we could eat."

I stood there quietly, feeling curiously suspended in space. Davy offered kindness with the same faith as a child. I could not refuse him.

"Where would we go?"

Davy's face relaxed a little.

"Somewhere not too pricey."

"We could eat at home."

Davy shook his head, all earnestness.

"I want to take you out for a meal."

We settled for a small Italian restaurant in Notting Hill Gate, nearly empty in the early evening. Inside the restaurant the flowers he'd given me, almost an embarrassment, were kindly and unexpectedly taken away by a matronly waitress and put in water until the meal was over. We studied the menu carefully for something which would not bruise our fragile finances. We both decided on lasagne with a large green salad to share between us. Davy ordered two pints of lager and then we sat in silence, unsure of what to say.

"Won't you forgive me?" Davy asked suddenly.

Bewildered, I looked down into my lap. I'd never realised forgiveness could be so difficult.

"What do you want me to say?" Davy's voice wavered. "I can't say it didn't happen because it did. You don't want me to lie to you."

I cleared my throat.

"How many others are there?"

Davy sat back.

"He's just a friend, Don. A Spanish boy. He calls by now and then. There's nothing in it."

"You sleep with him?"

"Now and then. Like I said, he calls. I didn't know he was coming round. It wasn't planned.

Davy seemed genuinely confused by my hurt. Perhaps my expectations of faithfulness were unreal to him. He was so much older than I. Maybe in a decade and a half I would have had a hundred lovers instead of just one. Maybe then I would believe going to bed with someone casually didn't matter, couldn't hurt.

I sat very still.

"When he came round, just by chance, why didn't you send him away?"

Davy looked dumbfounded.

"He's a friend. He brings a bottle of wine. We have a chat and a few glasses. Sometimes we fall into bed. It's only natural."

It was *me*, I thought. Somehow it was *my* fault.

"But you gave up Rob?"

"That was different. I saw a lot of him. The Spanish boy only appears once in a while."

There was a pause.

"Will you send him away next time?"

"Maybe." Davy's voice flared, a tiny flame fanned by my demands. "I have to be free, lad. It's not likely I'll be married now. I don't need ties."

"But what about me?"

"I can't help your hurt."

Davy swallowed his words as the waitress brought us our lasagne and salad.

"Let's eat, Don. Save the talk for later."

But I knew that this could never be resolved, only put aside. If Davy had been more articulate maybe we would have discussed everything further. Or perhaps we would only have used a greater vocabulary to further deceive ourselves. Maybe it was absurd to put more faith in words than feelings. Playing with the food, swallowing a little, I pushed pasta round my plate.

"Don't be sad, boy."

Looking into Davy's face, I was aware of his concern, the tenderness more tangible than words.

"You know you're special, Don."

Falling, I saw it was simple really, painfully straightforward. If I allowed myself to smile, I could have his arms holding me again, find him close beside me in the dark. But first of all I had to still the persistent questions and put my hurt aside, bury it.

When we left the pub we'd visited after the restaurant,

Davy, emboldened by the beer, ran his hand quickly along my forearm, bringing the lover to the surface. I couldn't help smiling.

"That's better," Davy said. "It worries me when you look so sad."

Giving in to silence, we walked on down the dirty London street, hesitant, bumping against each other like small children uncertain of our way. As we reached the junction where we would follow separate paths, we became solemn.

"I'll be off home, then," Davy said. "Get an early night."

Helpless, I shifted from one foot to another, swinging my bouquet, unconsciously pantomiming an unwanted bride. More than anything I wanted to Davy to hold me.

"I'll ring you tomorrow at work. Okay, lad."

Perhaps he was relieved to part from me. He glanced quickly down the street. Two men passing by on our side of the road made him afraid to be seen taking my hand.

"See you then."

He began walking down the road away from me, a retreating figure, looking back just once to wave. Watching him, remembering the Spanish boy, I realised I could not be certain he was going to end the evening alone. From now on I would never be sure.

6

THE SANDOWNE Guest House was set back from the road in a long quiet avenue. Before the large, pebble-dashed house was a wide squarish garden, discreetly hedged with roses and split by a winding gravel driveway, guarded by squat shrubs in white cement urns. The leaded windows were diamond-paned with clean white frames and red tile ledges. In the broad entrance porch deeper red geraniums in small cream tubs stood on the red tile floor.

"You can smell the sea from here," Davy said, as I rang the bell.

The green-painted door with its brass numbers and wide brass letterbox was opened confidently by a tall, elderly woman with white hair secured in a business-like bun.

"Mrs Harris?"

She nodded. "You are the gentlemen that telephoned earlier?"

"That's right." I smiled politely, aware of Davy shifting behind me with his bag.

It had all been arranged at the last minute. Both of us had taken the Monday off work. Davy had suggested Bournemouth and a long weekend break on the coast.

Mrs Harris smoothed her hands over her white and blue check apron.

"A double-room, wasn't it?" she enquired.

"Yes."

I hoped I sounded sure of myself. Mrs Harris seemed kindly

enough, but I couldn't help wondering if she was secretly worried about having homosexuals in her neat and tidy house. Maybe she naively believed that we were just friends. Most likely she had seen it all and was simply glad of the business.

"There is a room, as I said." Mrs Harris stepped back from the doorway, her welcoming smile a little worn at the edges after nearly three months of the holiday season. "Do come in."

It was the first room I'd ever felt was *ours*. There were two beds, one double and one single, parked a proper eighteen inches apart. It made me smile; separate beds, but one bed big enough for two to share. The walls of the room were painted a subdued cream and the worn carpet swam with flowers. Floral curtains were drawn back from discreetly veiled windows. The furniture – a wardrobe, a deep chest of drawers and a small dressing-table in front of the bay window – were all a dark, almost red wood, reminding me of my grandmother's house.

Davy, restless, came and stood behind me, his lips soft on the back of my neck. Turning to make the embrace whole, I put my arms around him. We kissed nervously, a quick brushing of our lips before Davy squeezed my hands and stepped away.

"What do you think?"

"It's grand."

"I suppose."

"The town's so clean after London. And peaceful. No screaming traffic or reggae thumping from two doors away." I would have carried on enthusiastically, but Davy was taking the bottle of gin and carton of orange juice out of the plastic bag which held our hastily purchased supplies. Scanning the room he picked up two glass beakers, one from either side of the old-fashioned porcelain hand-basin with its polished brass taps. I didn't want to drink then, but Davy smiling, handed me a beaker – half-gin, half-orange juice. Forcing myself, I swallowed quickly, coughing because it was strong and I was unused to the taste.

"Drink it up," Davy said. "You'll get to like it."

Draining his glass, he poured himself another gin and orange. It was only then I realised how completely ill at ease he was in the boarding-house room. Turning his face from me, he busied himself unpacking, taking his clothes out of the holdall and refilling his glass.

"More?" he offered.

"I'm fine."

Wishing it was different, I walked helpless to the window, pulling at the white net curtains to look out onto the gardens below me, the roses and the trees. I could not help myself wishing that this was my room, my house, my garden.

The double-bed grumbled under Davy's weight. Shifting into the middle of the mattress, he reached out a hand as I turned to face him.

"Come here, lad."

I did as I was told, climbing onto the bed and sitting astride him. Immediately he began undoing the belt of my trousers. Empty of desire I watched his fingers pulling at my shirt.

Too quickly, with barely a kiss and still wearing half our clothes, we made love quite lovelessly. For the first time, instead of wanting to prolong the embrace, I was relieved when he'd finished with me. Turning over to one side of the bed, I watched him quickly fall into a shallow doze.

"We can't use the bathroom together." Davy took a towel from his bag and stood up decisively. "It would look suspicious, both of us at once."

I wanted to protest, but then we heard children's voices outside the hall, the family next door. The sounds of other people, other guests, intruded. Without another word Davy left me, towel over one shoulder.

Clean and smelling of soap, I sat at the dressing-table and

dried my hair with a thick towel. Pausing, I could see Davy in the mirror still naked, putting his fresh clothes on the bed as if he were a soldier laying out his kit.

Aware I was watching him, Davy sought my reflection in the dressing-table mirror and smiled. Returning the smile I sat there waiting, hoping he would come to me. Instead he screwed the top back on the gin bottle.

"Let's go to the beach," he said. "We've been here hours and not seen the sea."

A sudden shower had cleared the beaches of late-summer holidaymakers. Empty deck-chairs dotted the beaches in what had been family groups. As we walked down the steep path that led to the sea-front, the promenade, a grey flagstone path below, was deserted. Ahead of us the old battered pier jutted out like a long dark finger. Driven by the wind the sea broke onto the shore in furious white-crested breakers.

Davy and I had hardly spoken on the bus journey into town. Now we were here we drifted down the path out of step with each other.

"It's like a ghost-town," Davy said.

"It'll be better tomorrow, the weather. Sunshine it said on the radio."

Davy shrugged, strode on ahead of me.

"Do you want to walk by the shore?"

He shook his head glumly.

"I haven't the shoes for beaches."

"Davy ..."

Perhaps the sharp wind stole my words away. Davy carried on walking. Standing quite still, I watched him go and waited. He was nearly a hundred yards away now. Still he hadn't turned round to look for me. Perhaps he could go on taking stubborn steps until he was out of sight, leaving me behind. The gulls circled above me, crying out. Shivering, I put my hands in my pockets, wishing absently for a heavier coat, wondering how I could bring Davy back.

To escape the rain we retreated to the cinema and a holiday double-bill of Indiana Jones films. Afterwards, walking back from the bus-stop we were silent under the glittering stars.

Back in our room I kissed him only to feel his mouth harden. Lowering my arms I let him go.

"We'll turn in, shall we?" Davy said. "I'm all worn out."

Yawning to emphasize his point, he considered the two beds.

"I'll take the small bunk." Davy sat down on the narrow bed, reinforcing his claim.

"As you wish, Davy."

We undressed in silence, without the smallest embrace, and quiet, we clambered into our separate beds.

At breakfast in the airy front room downstairs, we sat icily apart just like any couple who'd had a row the night before. Around us at the neat check-clothed tables sat two middle-aged couples and one young couple with small children, a boy and a girl. They all chatted about the weather and their plans for the day and seemed on familiar terms with each other. As Davy and I had entered the dining-room there had been a silence which, after a few glances in our direction, was swallowed bit by bit by small-talk.

Davy shyly kept his head down, mumbling politely as our landlady's daughter, a blonde woman in her late thirties, served us bacon and egg and marmalade and toast. We ate in silence. No one spoke to us and we were the first to leave.

Back in our room we took it in turns to clean our teeth at the pedestal basin, and then, with the extra care that comes after any disagreement, we kissed hesitantly, as well-mannered as relations. Davy clumsily squeezed my hand.

"I've upset you, lad."

Without answering, I leaned forward and kissed his forehead gently. He looked up at me.

"You know me, Don. I'm the hermit crab who likes his own shell best of all. It takes me a time to settle."

"I understand."

Davy dipped his head.

Gently, I touched his brow. He closed his eyes, accepting the touch. Then he turned his face and pressed his lips against my palm.

"I'm sorry," he said.

"Don't be. Please, Davy."

"I don't deserve you."

He looked up at me, for once completely open. His vulnerability made me reach out.

Then the early morning cleaner knocked at our door.

Stepping away from me, Davy smiled.

"Let's get ready for the beach."

On the way to the seafront we wandered across a wood that fringed a wide, undulating golf-course. The shimmering green grass drew us out of the shadows cast by branches into the sunshine.

"I would be romantic," Davy said, playfully. "But people might be watching."

"Sure, the golfers are really under-cover police."

"You never know."

"Davy."

We laughed at each other. I was suddenly happy.

"It's beautiful here."

"Not missing the city."

"Not one bit."

Davy watched my face carefully.

"Why, lad, I thought London was beautiful when I first arrived. It was like I'd come out of the sticks into the centre of everything. The glittering theatre-boards off Piccadilly seemed like magic. And the Strand and Shaftesbury Avenue, they'd only been names before, and suddenly I was there walking down them. So much seemed to be going on. Hustle and bustle. All those people going places."

"And where did you go?"

"A club or two, some gay. Someone tried to buy me once with real money. I was so angry. I told him I didn't do it for cash."

"Everybody needs company."

Davy shrugged.

"I met a nice man once at the Salisbury. He was so nervous, just like me. We kept looking and looking at one another, both of us too scared to say a peep. In the end I bought him a drink, took it over, my hands shaking like crazy, Don. He was a David like me."

Davy sighed, remembering, and I shivered because his past excluded me, made me a stranger.

"How long were you together?"

"Just the once. He gave me his telephone number, but I lost it. We had just that weekend at his house in Ealing. I used to go back to the Salisbury looking for him. He was never there."

We walked up a green slope towards a line of Lombardy poplars, silver-trunked and tall as soldiers.

"What about at sea, Davy? When you were in the merchant navy?"

Davy raised his hand to shield his eyes from the sun which was brighter even than yesterday's weathermen had predicted.

'I pretended I was straight more often than not. Took a woman on shore like the others. There was the odd boy in the bunk, but sometimes months without a soul. I remember one lad with red hair. Billy. Somewhere I've a snapshot of him."

"Were you ever in love?"

Davy frowned.

"With Geoff at the start maybe. Years ago now. I met him

on my first ever visit to London, in a public lavatory. You had to watch these places, be careful even then, but Geoff had a nice voice. Very gentlemanly. Like me he was shy of going to the pubs, all that standing and staring."

"So what happened to you and Geoff?"

Davy frowned.

"He got jealous. Wanted all of me just like Rob did. One time we had a terrible row. Not a peep for six months." Davy shrugged. "Still, we're friends again now."

Davy chatted on and I nodded and smiled, all the time thinking of one name. Geoff.

I have a photograph still of Davy up to his knees in the breaking sea. He is wearing light blue swimming-trunks and looking down, arms spread to balance himself against the waves. Out of focus, the figure is blurred, the face almost featureless, but curiously it captures Davy's vulnerability. Another photograph pressed under cellophane in my album is one Davy took of me up to my shoulders in water. I'd swum out a way, buffeted by the waves, before I turned round, wet-haired, to the shore. Too far away to be more than a dark shape among the grey blue breakers, one arm lifted in a wave.

If I close my eyes now and look back, remembering, I can again see Davy on the bright beach, a pale figure with a camera, melting in with the other holidaymakers drawn to the glittering water by the hot sun. I can hear the buzz of voices, the chatter, the calls of children rising with the rush of waves. Buoyant in the bracing water, I can recall my simple pleasure in floating on my back, my longing for Davy to join me, my bruised surprise that he couldn't swim.

I remember diving to impress him, kicking my legs just once to reach the rock-floor before surfacing jubilant with a stone. Shivering as I emerged from the sea, I can still see

Davy self-consciously stepping towards me with a towel. He slapped my back as we walked awkwardly up the beach together, the sting of shingle under our bare feet.

We took our time oiling each other's backs, kneading with firm fingers, our only allowed intimacy in the public eye. Afterwards we dozed on our towels, relaxed now that there seemed to be no need for conversation. Our blood drew us together, our desire teased by the sun. There is a deliciousness in knowing one wants to touch and that later, in a cooler place, you will make love.

That evening I cried out under Davy's hands, my shoulders and back burnt by the sun. Touching with extra care, we were tender and slow with one another, recapturing the sense of delight and discovery of our first time. Lying together in the wide bed, sticky with each other's sex, we were afraid to break the silence. A cool breeze blew through the half-open window, lifting the white net curtains like a ghost and goosepimpling our arms. I kissed Davy's chin.

"This could be us, every morning."

Lazily, Davy turned to look at me.

"What's that?"

Kissing the back of his neck, I eased myself closer to him, rubbing a palm flat down his thigh.

"Mrs Milosevic is throwing me out soon. Her relatives are coming earlier than she thought."

Davy sat up.

"You're not moving in."

Immediately I drew my whole body away. Davy reached over and took my hand.

"Do I sound hard, Don?"

"Yes."

"It was what you were asking."

"I didn't ask anything."

"Don, we can't share a tiny bed-sit."

"I don't want us to." I turned and faced him. "Together we

could get a flat. More than one room anyway."

Davy's mouth set in an obstinate line.

"It wouldn't work."

"It would if we both wanted it."

Naked together, suddenly we were close to fighting. Davy climbed out of bed away from me, running his fingers through his curly blonde hair.

"I've tried it once, lad. I'm sorry, but never again. We'd hate each other in a fortnight."

"It would be different for us."

"Why?"

"Because I'm different. I'm not the man you lived with before."

Davy sneered.

"So you won't be jealous when I don't come home? You won't ask where I've been?"

"But if you love me...?"

"Boy, you don't know where love stops."

"*It doesn't stop.*"

"*Nonsense, boy. Bloody romance.*"

"*No...*"

We were both shouting, our faces strained, scarred by what we'd said.

7

MY SUMMER finished as quickly as it had begun. An Indian sun burned away an unusually warm September and October crept in cold and cheerless. Autumn is seldom lovely in London. There are few trees except for those shut away in parks, and the fall of red and gold leaves can pass unmarked in a concrete city. You hurry out of work and find at the end of a crowded journey on the underground that the city has been plunged into a premature wintry darkness. Only at weekends do you have time to see the beauty of a crystal blue autumn sky frosted with grey cloud or stretched clear and empty.

I lived in Chelsea now in what must have been one of London's smallest self-contained flats, squeezed into a cramped but respectable mews house. My very own kitchen was less than a metre wide and only six feet deep. My bathroom, just as miniature, was only a toilet really with a small hand-basin and a mirror screwed onto the wall. When I first stood in the bed-sitting room I saw that the bed would have to be taken out. With barely room to swing a kitten the raised single-bed took up all the space that was left by the essential chest of drawers and tiny table. The "wardrobe" was a waist-level rail hidden in a corner behind a dusty curtain. To take the chill off the room there was an inefficient whirring fan-heater.

But it was somewhere to live.

With the bed taken out I put the narrow mattress on the

floor with a folded duvet on top. A red covering blanket and some black cushions a girl at work had given me transformed my bed into a floor-level settee.

Despite having a bathroom of my own, how to have a proper head-to-toe wash was something of a mystery. Lurking on a high shelf in the thin hallway was the biggest washing-up bowl you've ever seen, about three feet in diameter and eighteen inches deep. It was this bowl I stood in to have a shower, after placing it strategically on the bathroom floor to catch the drips from a rudimentary rubber shower faucet, its ends fitted over the taps of the tiny hand-basin. The whole process on a cold autumn evening, shivering exposed under drips of water with my feet in the broadest of bowls, was like a bizarre form of self-abuse.

The giant bowl, however, did have a secondary function. Living in exclusive SW3 I discovered that there was not one launderette close to hand. Perhaps the council thought they would lower the tone of the area. So I took to filling my enormous white bowl twice a week, kneeling on the toilet floor to wash out my shirts and smalls. My mother would have been proud of me.

"What you need," Davy said. "is another lover."

We were sitting inside a coffee-bar in the Bayswater Road. Two foaming cappucinos were brought to us by a handsome young Greek waiter wearing a tight white shirt and tighter black trousers.

"Nice bum," Davy said, admiring the rear view as the waiter walked away.

"I've seen better." I even smiled. Since the seaside weekend I'd tried to keep the hurt out of my voice. With practice, I told myself, I could weather anything.

"You should get yourself out and around more," Davy admonished. "Young lad like you. Find yourself someone."

I looked down into my creamy coffee. My twenty-fourth birthday had been a week ago. Kerry and Jan, two girls from work, had taken me out for a Chinese meal. Davy had been busy.

"If I took a lover," I persisted, "you'd only be hurt. You know you would."

Davy made a face. "I would not. Not if you didn't get too friendly with them." He stirred his coffee round and round with a spoon, then glanced at me quickly. Reaching across the red and white checkered formica table, he laid his hands palm down a permissible inch away from mine.

"You were good this morning," he said. "Very good."

"Am I meant to shout about it?"

"You could get a lover easy. Being good in bed you'll keep him."

"Like I've kept you."

"Exactly." Never suspecting irony, Davy smiled sideways at me, rapped his hands on the table as if something had been settled.

Sitting back on the hard bench seat, I sipped my hot coffee without any pleasure.

'So it's an eye for an eye.'

Davy frowned.

"Why quote the bible at me?"

"If I have another lover, we're equal, Davy. That's what you're telling me. If I have Fred and Harry that makes up for your Geoff and the Spanish boy."

"There's no one else."

"Besides Geoff and the Spaniard."

Davy paused. "Geoff and I have been friends for years. Fancying doesn't come into it."

"But bed does?"

"We all need sex. Geoff as much as you or I. A friend can oblige."

"And the Spanish boy whose name you can't even remember?"

"I only see him now and then," Davy protested. "And you know I've no memory at all."

I was meant to smile, but instead I sat up. "You sit there, Davy, so concerned and tell me I should be unfaithful because you feel guilty two-timing me."

"There's no guilt."

"*No...*" My voice wavered. Suddenly I was weary of all this. Leaden-faced, I was aware of Davy frowning, at once trying to read my thoughts and shut out my accusing silence.

"I want to be free, that's all," he said. "I can't be caged like those little birds."

"Budgerigars."

"I'll never live with anyone. I told you that. I need space. Then there's my family to consider. What would Da say if he knew?"

"His eldest son is a poofter, I should think he'd hang himself."

Davy's silence reprimanded me, but immediately I was ashamed. I really hadn't thought it would come to this. Finding Davy, loving for the first time; suddenly such a feeling was there that I'd believed we'd both be transformed, that the world would change almost, somehow be a brighter place.

"I'm sorry, Davy." Putting my hands palm down beside his hands, I copied the gesture he'd made to me earlier. In the quiet of that moment the tenderness of our very first meeting was recalled, a curious echo of what had once been. Davy's face was suddenly calm as if this situation, strange to me, was familiar to him. But then, he'd probably been through all this before.

"No need to be sorry, lad." He hesitated. "I'll be the one who drives you away."

Again I had the sense of Davy remembering, his expression curiously resigned. Yet in his voice was there the wish that this time things might be different?

Davy looked at me sadly, his grey eyes unexpectedly full of asking. I've never known anyone who could appear to love so genuinely without being aware of the contradictions they imposed. Or was the controversy of my making? Davy loved simply, without acknowledging faithfulness or constancy. Could I say his love was less than mine?

We stood up, for some reason caught in the web of emotion we'd knitted between us. Our hearts trembling under our winter coats, we hid behind gestures; tying our scarves, stacking the cups and saucers. It was as though we were standing close to an edge. One more clumsy step and it would all be over. We hesitated.

"I'll never leave you," I said.

"Who says I want you to?"

We glanced at one another shyly, joined for just a moment without embrace. Davy shifted his feet.

"I've the bill to pay."

"Let me treat you."

"No. My treat." Davy ambled self-consciously to the counter where the moustachioed Greek waiter stood in his tight black trousers. Handing the loose bill to the young man, Davy reached in his back pocket for his wallet. He turned to me half-whispering as the waiter stepped sideways to the cash-till.

"I'll buy him for you if you want," Davy murmured. "Just say and he's yours."

An old love song blared in the background of the crowded pub. Perhaps I was the only one listening, my eyes to the floor, following the words of the song in my head. Everyone else was either chattering, glancing round hoping to catch someone's eye, or standing silent, drink in hand, looking and waiting. It was Friday night and everyone was hoping extra hard that they would find either love or a satisfying fuck before the weekend was over.

Davy was at Geoff's comfortable flat in Kentish Town. He was spending the whole weekend there watching the specially inported videos on Geoff's deluxe video recorder. 'You should come along,' Davy had said. 'Geoff's been wanting to meet you for ages. The three of us could share a bed. It could be fun, lad...Why not try it..?'

I wondered if Davy would ever see how such words hurt.

But here I was in the pub on my own, trying to blot out so many thoughts. It was strange. My first time in a gay pub I'd felt so uncomfortable and isolated. Tonight the bar was a sort of refuge. Even though no one was speaking to me, I was in some way supported by the presence of other gay men. In one sense among my own kind, I felt less lonely and more relaxed here than in my solitary bed-sit. Leaning back against a beamed wall, I ran my eyes quickly round the men standing in the bar. Still I wished Davy was here with me.

The pub grew even more crowded. Catching sight of a good space in the corner, I took a step forward and almost walked into the arms of a short, well-built young man with a pale face and straight black hair. His dark eyes stared, then shied away.

"I was coming to talk to you," he said, "I'm Peter."

Strangely formal, he held out his hand, then took it away quickly when I did not instantly complete the handshake. Flushing, he glanced at me sideways.

"Can I get you a drink?"

"Lager, thanks."

"What's your name?"

"Donovan."

"That's unusual."

"Mostly people call me Don."

"Don, then."

He smiled uncertainly, then made his way to the bar. I

wondered if he was a visitor to the capital. His clothes seemed too conservative for a Londoner – corduroys and Nature-Trek shoes, an unflattering square-cut anorak. When he came back with the drinks I noticed his hands were shaking.

"I've never seen you here before."

He shook his head quickly.

"I don't go to places like this. Not often, anyway. What about you?"

"Now and then." I took a swallow of beer. "You work in London?"

"I'm between jobs at the moment." He turned his head as he said this as though covering up a lie. Draining his tumbler of whisky in one greedy swallow, he took a step closer to me.

"You look nice," he said. "Nice as a person. Not like the others here."

Something in his voice made me uneasy.

"They're not as bad as you think." I tried to sound reassuring. "No one's going to jump on you."

Peter giggled.

"You are nice."

Bewildered, I looked away across the bar and, immediately, felt Peter reach for my free hand. He squeezed my fingers tightly, just as a child might seek reassurance. Only he had the strong grip of a man.

"Another drink, then?" He pursed his lips.

"It's my round."

I tried to reach into my pocket for some coins, but instead of letting go of my hands, he tightened his grip painfully, just like a playground bully.

"Let me get the drinks," he said. "Please."

And he let my hand go. Part of me wanted to walk away then, but I stood my ground, determined to appear perfectly calm. And he was physically attractive. Perhaps in the back of my mind the thought of Geoff and Davy together made me want to stay.

"Just a half-pint."

"A half, then," he said, softly.

His momentary belligerence wiped away, he grinned as though we were friends before he moved to the bar. He returned with a full pint, glancing at me quickly, daring me to refuse it. As soon as I'd taken the beer from him, he took my free hand again.

"Do you live close by?" he asked.

"Not far away."

"You live on your own."

"Yes." I was too slow to lie.

"Can we go there?"

"You're going too fast..."

Instantly he let my hand go, stepped backward, his hurt transparent like a child's.

"You don't want me." He sounded lost.

"Not like this. Peter ..."

Ignoring me, he turned away and quickly pushed a path through the press of people to the bar. Something in me, perhaps a sense of foreboding, stopped me from following him.

Within half an hour Peter was sitting on a middle-aged man's lap, putting his tongue in the man's ear. Something about the picture they made was grotesque. Both their faces were flushed with amusement. The big man, in a studded leather jacket, sat laughing as he jogged Peter up and down on his knee like a bizarre ventriloquist's dummy.

Later, when I came back from the Gents, both Peter and the man had gone. Uneasy, I made my way back to the bar, getting a pint just before the bell for last orders.

He was sitting on the steps of a tall Victorian house, his head in his hands, crying.

"Peter?"

Looking up wildly, he shivered as he recognised me, and turned his wet face away.

"What's happened?"

"Nothing."

"Are you all right?"

He wiped his eyes with his hands.

"Leave me alone."

Glancing anxiously up at the front-door of the house, I half-expected lights to come on and a complaint at the disturbance.

"You can't stay here," I said.

"Where else can I go?"

"Home."

"Home is twenty miles away. I'm too drunk to drive back."

If he was lying about where he lived, he certainly was in no state to drive anywhere. And whatever I thought I couldn't leave him here.

"You'd better come home with me."

He wiped his eyes again. Calm, as though there hadn't been tears a moment ago, he glanced up into my face with that intense stare as if he could see right under my skin.

Five minutes from my tiny flat, as we were stepping down a dimly-lit side street, he suddenly stepped in front of me. Before I could move back, he grabbed both my wrists with his hands. Again I was aware of the strength in his grip. As I turned to face him, he licked his lips.

"Will you kiss me?"

"No..."

'I could make you."

"Maybe." I took a sharp breath.

"I know what you're thinking." He tightened his grip, pinning my arms to my side.

Tense, I wondered how I would get free of him.

"You're thinking...if I take him home he might smash up the place."

"I'd stop you."

Peter smiled, his face pale in the dark.

"I'm stronger than you. You know that. Could you guess how many hours I've spent in the gym..."

I tried to push my fear away.

"I'm trying to help you, Peter."

He stood very still, his breath smoky in the cold air. He released his grip a little.

"It's up to you." I tried to sound firm. "You can stay out here all night and freeze on the streets if that's what you want."

He let me go then reached for my hand again, held it very gently.

"You can trust me," he said.

Inside my tiny Chelsea flat I made tea which he hardly touched. Silent, we both stripped modestly down to our underpants and turning off the light, lay down under the duvet, forced close together on the single mattress. Peter reached behind him for my nearest arm which he lay across his broad chest. We shifted ourselves slowly, an inch at a time, not speaking until he lay comfortably in my arms.

"Have you anyone?" he asked, after a while.

"Sort of. A Welshman. We're very different ..."

"Does he love you?"

"I don't know."

Peter stroked my arm.

"I think you're lucky," he said. "I can tell."

He pressed his back close to me, moving for a moment before at last he settled. For a long time I held him while the clock on the floor beside me ticked past the minutes. At last, I heard him sigh like a child finally falling into a dream.

When I woke in the morning, he was gone. Behind, he'd left a scribbled note by my pillow in slanting handwriting.

First time I ever shared a bed and nothing happened. It was nice. I only mess things up so I shall keep away. You and everyone are better off without me.

I can only wonder where Peter is now. I never saw him again.

8

I WAS in the middle of making chilli con carne, stirring in the tomatoes and kidney beans, when the bell in the hallway rang.

As I opened the front door, he glanced at me shyly. Turning back, I made my way up the stairs, hearing him shut the door and follow me, his footsteps heavy with uncertainty. In the narrow upstairs hallway, I avoided his face.

"Do you want coffee?"

"I've brought wine." Davy held up a bottle wrapped in purple tissue paper. "Liebfraumilch."

I remembered the meal he'd cooked me in his flat. There had been wine then and the flicker of candlelight on the table. Davy took a step closer.

"Perhaps we'll save the wine for later. Coffee'll be fine for now."

Shrinking from him, like someone bruised, I retreated to the kitchen to put on the kettle. Davy followed me. Between us we filled the cramped kitchen space. Gazing down at the grey linoleum floor, Davy took three deep breaths.

"I had to spend the weekend with Geoff."

I thought how I never wanted to hear that name again.

"Had to, Davy? Aren't you the free agent? Aren't you the man that won't be caged?"

"Don, Geoff asked me round. I couldn't refuse."

"It's easy, Davy. You just say 'No'."

Davy bit his lip.

"I wanted to see him."

Taking a breath, I tried to concentrate on pouring hot water from the kettle into two ridiculously bright mugs.

"How were the videos?"

"You're all upset."

He moved towards me and I took a step back, pressing myself against one wall.

"Davy, did I tell you you couldn't see Geoff this weekend?"

"No."

"Did I make a fuss about it?"

"Not really." Davy half-smiled nervously. "I never thought you minded."

"You never thought."

"Look now, I see you're upset. I'm sorry, Don, and I'm here to make it up to you."

"It can't be made up, Davy. We're different and we want different things. And it won't work."

Davy moved closer, uncertain about embracing me, but frightened by my words.

"Donovan, you know I care."

"Yes..."

'Well then, it'll be all right."

My face twisted.

"But you don't love me, Davy."

He stood quite still, not knowing how to face me. I could almost feel his confusion. He had to force himself to speak, his face flushed.

"You know I want you."

"But not enough, Davy."

He avoided my eyes.

"Your wanting all of me, lad, drives me away."

"*I can't bear you making love to someone else.*"

The silence in the small room then was like an explosion. I could see the darkness in Davy's eyes. We twisted away from each other. Then Davy spoke.

"If you found yourself a lover, someone for now and then, you wouldn't mind."

This was too old an argument.

"I want faithfulness, Davy. You don't."

"I could try ..."

Reaching out his arms, he moved to hold me, but afraid, I stepped away from him.

It's harder to fall out of life than most people think. The cycle of routine goes on and on. Whatever you feel, after more than a few hours, you are hungry or thirsty. There's soon shopping to do; milk, bread, coffee, cereal, sausages. And at the back of your wardrobe the pile of dirty washing grows everyday, spreading from one bag to two, until there are no clean socks, pants or shirts left, and a visit has to be paid to the laundrette. Everyday crockery is washed and dried and put away in cupboards and in drawers. You stand in front of a small mirror, your severed image thrown back at you, and shave and brush your teeth and comb your hair. You undress only to put on your clothes again. Sleep only to wake again. Eat simply to shit and eat again.

Work summons us with unwavering authority, without any regard to happiness. I went about my duties in the Dole Office smiling at the faces of the day, conducting civilised interviews, receiving, with a routine comment on the weather, the forms the members of the public returned. But Davy haunted every step. For the past fortnight those in the office had been going down with 'flu one by one. Finally the germs got to me. My whole body ached and my head swam. My boss, shaking his head, sent me home early with a temperature.

In the dim afternoon my cramped bed-sitting room smelled of damp. Even the whirring fan-heater couldn't dispell the cold air which hung over the walls in invisible chill curtains. With a mug of tea, I lay down on my mattress on the floor, pulling my duvet over me as I began to shiver.

Waking to darkness, I was summoned by the bell ringing in the hall. Hauling on my dressing-gown, I stumbled down the mews stairs, fumbled with the front door, only to discover Davy absurdly bearing gifts.

"I rang at work," he said. "They told me you were poorly, so here I am."

His cheerful concern made me want to cry with frustration.

"I'm not sure if I want you here, Davy."

He looked at me steadily, his grey eyes reproaching me for my hurt. Under one arm, he supported a potted plant with large feathery pink flowers.

"A cyclamen." He put the plant-pot firmly into my arms in such a way that not taking it would have meant it falling and smashing on the front doorstep.

"You'd better come in, then."

Stepping back from the doorway to make room for him, tears of weakness filled my eyes.

"That's the ticket, lad." Davy gave me a quick smile. "I knew you'd be needing company."

Besides the cyclamen, Davy had brought me a half-bottle of whisky and some lemon-drink cold medication. Ushering me back under the duvet he stood in the middle of the cramped room and sighed.

"You should never have moved in here, Don. Hardly bigger than a coffin."

Lying on the mattress on the floor, I looked up at him as if he was a giant.

"If you'll remember Davy, I wanted things differently."

"So you did."

Dipping his chin, Davy moved away into the kitchen and made tea and the lemon cold-drink. He brought the mugs in and sat cross-legged on the floor beside me, spurning the room's one hard chair.

"You need a proper bed, Don."

"There's no room." Warmer under the duvet, comforted by having Davy so close, the creaking tension in my head eased a little.

"It'll be like an ice-box in winter."

"You do go on, Davy Davies."

"You'll get a chill on your chest if you stay here."

"Where else is there?"

The words hanging in the air made Davy nervous of my glance. I turned my face into the pillow. Reaching out, Davy ruffled my hair, then very slowly grazed the side of my face with his finger.

"You're sweating with fever, lad."

"Nearly a hundred degrees they said at work."

"Perhaps we should get you a doctor."

"I'm not dying, Davy. It's just the 'flu."

Davy nodded and carried on stroking my face, while I lay still.

"Maybe you could stay with me." Davy's voice strained with hesitancy. "Just for a few days mind, until you get better."

My heart turned to a hard fist in my chest. It was Davy's way to undo his own good, trimming kindness with caution. It was Davy's way...He would never change. A tear rolled unevenly down my cheek, trickling over my lips onto the pillow.

Unaware, Davy sat beside me as the room sank further into darkness. Wiping my eyes, I reached out an arm from under the covers to take Davy's hand. He trembled.

"Are you cold?"

"That's another thing this room could do with, Don. Central heating."

I sighed. "There's hardly enough room for a radiator."

"True enough." He shivered again.

"If you're cold come under the duvet."

Davy smiled feebly. "I was wondering when it would come to that."

"You don't have to stay."

My voice strained, I turned my face up to the single window and the square of sky, the deepest blue before night.

"What about it, coming to stay with me for a few days?"

My heart twisted.

"Perhaps ..."

My voice trailed away hopelessly. Silence filled the room with a hollow sense of ending. Davy sat unmoving for a long time. Then he stood up self-consciously, stretching out his arms, glancing to the solitary window just like someone trapped. If Love could secure and make good freedom, it could not grant it. Those first uncertain steps had to be taken on your own.

"We'll have the whisky soon," Davy said. "I'll put it with some hot milk."

Struggling out of his sweater and shirt, Davy unbuckled his belt and stepped out of his jeans, a lean silhouette. For a moment he knelt beside me. I lifted the duvet for him. Silently he moved down onto the narrow mattress, the backs of his legs cold against my thighs. Putting my arms around his chest, I held him closely, tenderly brushing the back of his neck with my lips. Gradually the tension in his body eased and he lay relaxed, one arm reaching behind to touch me, making sure I was there.

"I haven't been good for you, have I?"

His words echoed, quiet resignation in his voice. Again the tears welled in my eyes.

"I could say the same, Davy."

He shook his head.

"I knew what you wanted, lad. From that first night at the club, I saw it. You were after love."

He trembled in my arms, turning over to face me. For the

first time he saw my tears. As though he'd never seen anyone cry, he reached out and wiped a tear gently away with his fingertip. When he spoke his voice was a whisper.

"Let me stay tonight."

Another tear ran slowly down my face. Davy traced its path with a finger, then sighing, he nestled closer to me and closed his eyes.

For a long time I held him, while the tears silently stained my face.

9

"DO YOU want a buttermilk bedroom? Or would you prefer a Harmony or a Misty shade?"

Davy smiled.

"You choose," he said.

We were standing inside a high street do-it-yourself store in front of a bright display of paint colours.

"You found the flat," I said, carefully.

Davy turned to me.

"It's for *our* bedroom."

Our. The word was somehow comforting. I ran my eyes once again over the colour cards.

"Perhaps we ought to get paint that fits in with the carpet and curtains." I turned my attention back to Davy. "What colour are they under all that dust?"

For a moment I thought Davy hadn't heard me. His face was suddenly blank as though he were somewhere else. Perhaps it was the strangeness of these last days, the suddenness of the changes ...

Davy had discovered the flat tucked away at the bottom of a tall, crumbling Victorian house in Queen's Park. It was a decent size, having a large lounge, a double bedroom and a separate kitchen and bathroom. There was even a small garden at the back. The reason we could afford it was because of the run-down condition it was in.

As you entered the dim hallway the smell of damp and cats almost knocked you over. In the narrow kitchen the crooked cupboards were coming away from the walls covered with dirt and grease. The gas-cooker, practically an antique, looked as though a hundred saucepans had boiled over and still no one had cleaned up.

Although the previous tenant, a Mrs Wheeler, was no longer in occupation, she'd left traces of her life behind her. The stick she'd used, perhaps to support her stumbling walk, still stood in the corner of the living room beside the heavily indented armchair which must have been her favourite resting place. On the mantelpiece above the old-fashioned gas-fire pranced a set of brown and white china dogs grey with dust.

But dust was everywhere. The windows were grimy and the veiled curtains discoloured. Faded floral wallpaper was coming away from the walls and spider-webs had collected in the corner of the ceilings. Everywhere bore the marks of the helpless neglect of an old woman too frail or infirm to make the necessary practical changes and repairs. It was difficult to believe that the flat would ever feel like home.

Coming out of his own private reverie, Davy seemed to read my thoughts.

"Once we've decorated the bedroom, it'll be all right," he said. "Then we'll have at least one liveable room to sleep in."

That night we slept on a mattress on the living-room floor. We had worked together all afternoon and evening in the bedroom , stripping away all the old wallpaper.

Weary, we undressed for bed in darkness, lying down on the wide mattress without an embrace. With the two wardrobes towering over me and the walls of boxes and bags we still couldn't unpack, I felt as though I were sleeping on the floor of an old junk shop.

Restless, for a long time I lay awake, listening to the tick of Davy's old clock set on the mantelpiece where once the china dogs had been. It had taken four black dustbin liners to clear the flat of old Mrs Wheeler's personal possessions. Thinking of the old lady, imagining her sitting in the sagging armchair, I reached out to touch Davy who was sleeping with his back to me. But his body seemed to reject even the thought of a caress.

We'd argued that afternoon, irritated by the dust and dirt, sensitive to the fact that now we had to try and make it together; that neither of us had a separate space to escape to.

So began a routine. Every evening we came home from work and changed out of our working clothes into our oldest jumpers and jeans. After a quick cup of tea, we'd go back into the bedroom to continue our decorating.

First we had to finish stripping the peeling wallpaper off the ceiling and walls using solvent and metal scrapers. Then we sanded down all the woodwork; the window frame, the curtain rail, the door and the skirting boards. We'd left the calor-gas heater on full for days to try and dry the walls out, but in the end Davy had to chisel out the worst of the damp patches, damp-proof the walls and then replaster. Then we wallpapered everywhere and overnight the room was as white and bright as a room in a hospital.

Weary, hardly able to believe we would ever finish, we began the painting, undercoating the walls ready for two coats of the pale lilac paint Davy had chosen because it was a soft enough colour to encourage sleep.

Lilac dreams, I'd teased, and it became a catchphrase between us; something to make us smile when the dust, the plaster, the glue, the paper and the paint made us want to run out of the flat screaming.

Lilac dreams.

All we seemed to do was work on the flat.

Perhaps they were happy days? The sense of labour drew us closer, but also wore us down to the point of sadness. Tired, neither of us could hide our doubts. Had we done the right thing in living together? Since we'd moved into the flat we hadn't made love once, seldom ever kissed. Never have I understood why it was like that.

The evening after we'd finished painting our lilac walls Davy came home with a large brown paper parcel. Inside the package were new curtains; the palest cream background with feathery green leaves interlaced with lavender and pale blue flowers.

Still nervous of kissing me Davy stepped away. I held the curtains up between us, soft in my hands.

"They're beautiful."

"I chose the material 'specially. You're always going on about flowers, and I've hardly bought you any."

Not knowing what to say, I took his hand.

"You'll see the blue and purple blooms," Davy whispered, "Last thing at night and first thing in the morning. All year round."

At last the day came when everything in the bedroom was done. Scarcely able to believe we'd finished, we took it in turns to soak in a hot-scented bath. Sitting up in bed with tall glasses, the room warmed by the gas-fire, we shared a bottle of red wine.

For days we hadn't touched, but when at last he held me I was happy. At the keenest moment of shared pleasure there was for once no ending. Wet in our embrace, still we lay in each other's arms.

Davy kissed me.

"I love you," he whispered.

It was the only time he ever used those words. But I cannot forget.

Living together involved unforeseen changes and compromise, and the loss of what we both called our independence. We argued, sometimes bitterly. Perhaps love, if it endures, makes us responsible. But it takes time to get used to, this business of considering someone else's needs.

I was often afraid, but gradually the fear faded and there

were times when I felt more content and secure than ever before. At the end of the day I lay down to sleep with my lover beside me. And when I woke in the morning and reached out, he was there.

In the moments of doubt, it was strangely the small routine things which helped reassure me. Cooking for the first time became satisfying now I was preparing a meal for both of us. Ironing, previously so tedious, had a relaxing even theraputic quality, now my life had a calmer home base. And of course, if I ironed his shirts, then a week later I could sit and watch him take his turn at the ironing-board.

Even shopping for groceries, a chore I'd always disliked, was almost enjoyable now we wheeled a trolley round Sainsbury's together, treating ourselves occasionally to favourite cheeses and biscuits, selecting a joint of meat for a shared Sunday roast.

My one regret was that we didn't spend Christmas together that year. I went home to Mum and Dad and Davy took the train back to Wales, spending the festive season with his Da and his brother's family in Blaengarw."There'll be other Christmases for you and me," Davy said.

The New Year came and went. The winter weeks slipped by and gradually the darkness didn't draw in quite so soon. I was able to walk about the flat in one jumper instead of two. When March came, I turned my attention out of doors.

The garden of our basement flat was small and U-shaped; overgrown flowerbeds around an oblong of rakishly tall grass.

"There's some shears in the hall cupboard," Davy said, one Sunday afternoon. "I could cut the lawn back."

"It's better if we clear the beds, first. Uproot all the weeds."

Davy nodded.

"Right then."

Several mugs of tea and six black dustbin liners later, the flowerbeds were two-thirds clear of weeds, bramble and dead plants.

"We'll save the smelly part 'till next week," I said. "Digging in the horse-manure."

Davy grinned.

"Are you sure you know what you're doing?"

"I've seen my mother put manure in the ground for roses. It must enrich the soil."

"Feeding the earth before the plants feed themselves."

"That's the logic of it."

Standing close to him, I reached out a hand to touch his cheek, then stopped , remembering the neighbours. You only had to step out into the backyard before the curtains twitched.

Davy winked at me.

"We deserve a rest and a cup of tea," he said.

"Sounds good."

We smiled at one another and I was aware of Davy standing close behind me.

"I'll run the hot water," he whispered. "If you'll share a bath with me."

As I began to trust Davy, so the sex between us grew better and better. Secure in his arms, at last I could relax completely, put aside my fear of being held, my body at another's mercy. Whatever anyone says, being fucked by another man can be the most miserable of sexual experiences. But it can also be an experience which is profoundly pleasurable. Being able to satisfy each other in this way deepened our sense of sharing, as though now nothing was being held back.

Of course at the time when Davy and I shared this – not so very long ago – relatively few people in the United Kingdom had heard of AIDS. Even though a number of men had died in this country, it was still perceived very much as a North American disease. There was not yet the panic for Immunity, and Safe Sex meant only steering clear of the Yanks.

In barely a few months things would change.

For Easter we bought each other chocolate eggs. "The first I've had since I was a kiddy," Davy said.

I ruffled his hair.

"It's not Easter, not properly, without an egg."

Davy grinned.

"You're a weird one, boy."

Shrugging, I sat up.

"Why should we give things up just because we're adults? If we had children of our own we'd be playing at Christmas and Easter for years."

"You want babies now?"

I laughed. "Despite even your ingenuity, Davy, I don't think we could manage that."

Davy dipped his head, teasing. "Wait till we're married."

"Aren't we married now?"

"We're living together..." Davy made a face.

"It feels like being married."

"Being married is Church and Weddings, Don. Family celebration. It's different from this."

"But it comes down to living together."

"Maybe." Davy shook his head, smiled. "Next thing I know you'll be asking me for a ring."

The following Saturday morning I woke to discover a freak fall of April snow. Clearing a space on the cold frosty glass of the bedroom window, I looked out to see a thin white blanket covering everything in the backyard. In a sudden shaft of sunshine the snow glittered crisp and brilliant, making even our small garden beautiful.

I woke Davy with a kiss high on his forehead. He blinked, turning over playfully and hiding his head under the bed-covers.

"Davy, I've brought you tea."

Making doggy growling noises, he burrowed deeper under

the blankets. Smiling, I slipped off my dressing-gown and crept under the covers to join him, feeling him move close and wrap his arms around me, press his face into my chest.

"Mind where you put your cold feet," he whispered.

"You're as hot as toast."

"I want to stay that way." There was a laugh in his throat.

"Cuddle me," I asked.

"Cuddle me says the Ice-Box. Where did you get such cold hands?"

"There's snow outside. The kitchen's like a refrigerator. Frost on the window. I made us both a cup of tea."

"You deserve a hug then."

"Mmmm."

The snow disappeared as quickly as it had come. Spring was firmly settled in. Davy watched me fill the lightweight plastic trays with earth from the garden. Using a pencil to dig small holes, I painstakingly sowed one by one the seeds from the packets: night-scented stocks, lavender, pansies, lupins and mesembryantheums. Watering the trays using an old milk-bottle, Davy solemnly promised to buy me a watering-can. We covered the trays with wedge-shaped shards of glass left over from a once-broken window.

"If we leave these in the light and remember to water them," I said, "They should be all right."

Davy nodded.

"So all we need now is luck."

Now the days called to summer. The evenings grew lighter, drawing people out onto the streets. Everything was taking shape now. Davy had cut the grass back and raked out even the most persistent weeds. The seeds we'd planted under glass in the plastic trays, sprouted green tendrils and minature curls of leaf. Two weeks later the seedlings stood tall enough to plant out into the garden.

"It will be a fair splash of colour," Davy said, contemplating the flower-beds, imagining how it would be.

"We can sunbathe out here." I smiled at him. "Get a tan while we watch the flowers grow."

"And next year, roses."

"Yes."

We looked at one another, as though we were still surprised at our closeness. It was strange that sense of maybe having a future; the two of us together sharing a life.

In May we decorated the living-room, painting the walls white-with-a-hint-of-apricot. It made the flat brighter, gave us the feeling of having more space.

And the summer came.

In the warm evenings the air in our garden was sweet with the perfume of white and purple night-scented stocks. The sweet peas, delicate shades of red, blue and mauve, climbed the strings between the bamboo canes, became a wall of soft warm colour. The pansies were cheerful clown-faces and the common stocks stood sturdy cream and gold. Even the lavender flourished. The fiery mesanbryanthemum closed their daisy heads in early evening and opened again bright in the dawn.

In the hot July days the earth dried out and cracked and we feared the flowers would perish. So every evening, when the heat of the day had died away into an exhausted thrumming, Davy and I watered our garden. I'd stand in the kitchen and fix the suction end of the hose over the cold-water tap. The long hose snaked out through the kitchen window down to where Davy stood, waiting for the first jet of water. The flow of the water could be adjusted and Davy took great care, making sure that the frailest flowers were dampened by the finest spray.

Wandering out to the garden in light clothes, I'd stand close to him in the cool dark, caught in the long drawn cry of summer. As the droplets of water fell onto the flowers we'd

tended, above us were the stars, brilliant in the night sky. I'd
shut my eyes and just listen, aware of him there. Never have I
known such peace.

10

IT WAS Davy's idea to have a camping holiday. We borrowed a tent and sleeping bags from one of my friends at work, and splashed out on a hired car.

It took us the best part of the day to drive down from London to the Devon campsite. Although it was now late August and we'd had weeks of sunshine, rain dotted the windscreen of the borrowed Fiat as we left the dirty capital.

"It'll clear as we drive further south," Davy said, daring the weather to break.

Nodding agreeably, I sucked a Traveller's humbug, intent on the road atlas on my lap and my role as navigator.

We only lost our way once, after taking the wrong turning off a busy roundabout. Slipping off the road into the nearest lay-by, we shared a calming cup of tea from a thermos flask, before we set off again. We were both tired when, in the late afternoon, we at last bumped our way down the rutted lane leading to the high green field where we were to pitch our tent. Being the height of the British holiday season, caravans (some of them presumably resident, with solid wooden balconies and round tubs of plants) took up most of the site. The rest of the grassy area was taken over by the tenting community, most of whom were under thirty.

Negotiating a way round the tents and caravans we found a space in the bottom corner of the field, partially under the cover of trees. Davy thought the overhanging branches would help shelter us if it happened to rain. Having chosen our location, we unpacked the hollow metal poles that made up the tent-frame and the neatly folded blue canvas tent. Last Saturday we'd practised setting up the tent in the garden. Then, we'd worked leisurely, pausing to have a cup of tea in moments of uncertainty. Now, weary after the car journey, we attempted to erect the tent in record-breaking time. In the consequent confusion tempers flared again, and as my mother would have put it, "Words were said".

All this was to the amusement of a party of black teenage girls from Brixton who, under the cheerful supervision of a bespectacled adult, put up the group's four tents in the time it took us to try to fit the canvas over a frame which was upside down. It had taken us nearly two hours.

"You have to laugh," I said hopefully.

Davy cuffed my head.

"Just take your dearest to the pub," he said. "And get him a drink."

With a pint of beer in his hand, Davy's more relaxed expression showed that things were looking up. The pub we'd discovered, surrounded by hedge and a field where black and white cows grazed, served hot meals. Sitting comfortably with a pint, we both settled for a large well-done steak.

"We'll save the excitement of the calor-gas stove for tomorrow," Davy said, making a wry face.

"You can have first go in the morning, boiling up the water for tea."

"I knew we should have brought a teasmade."

"No excuse, I'm expecting my cup of tea in bed, same as usual."

"Ssh." Davy gave the locals in the saloon bar a cautious glance, and theatrically lowered his voice. "They might not have discovered poofs in Devon."

"But we get everywhere."

Davy smiled, the irritation of the tent-erecting hours

forgotten after our meal. He glanced at his wristwatch, then laughed at himself.

"I was thinking we could catch the News," he admitted. "But we've no telly."

"We don't need it. We can sit snugly up in our sleeping-bags reading."

Davy grinned.

"Educating me now, are you?"

I shrugged, defensively.

"Reading for pleasure, I meant."

Davy looked into my eyes.

"All right, Donovan. I'll give the books a try. If I get bored you can cuddle me."

"I'll drink to that."

A little unsteady on our feet, but definitely happy, we negotiated our way through the tents, narrowly avoiding tripping over guide-ropes in the dark.

"Tell the angels to put on the lights."

"I hope we find the right tent."

Davy nudged my arm.

"Ssh."

"Someone's singing."

And they were. High voices, rising and falling in unison, almost like a church choir except that they were singing not a hymn but a pop song. George Michael's *Careless Whisper*.

"It's the Brixton girls."

I reached out and held Davy's hand in the dark. For a moment longer the voices carried on in careful harmony, before a gruff voice sounded from a neighbouring tent.

"All right, girls. That's enough. Get some sleep."

Amid some giggles and the odd muttered expletive, the singing came to a stop.

Davy and I found our tent and, after fiddling with the knots, crept inside on our hands and knees. It took us ten minutes blind searching to find the torch.

"We'll know to leave it just inside the flap next time."

Lying back on the padded sleeping-bag, Davy reached out a hand, his eyes studying my face in the torchlight.

"Come over here," he whispered. "And give your old man a kiss."

The sun cast shafts of light down into the high-arched hall of the wood. The air was hot and still. Above us, leaves on the trees hung heavy and green like broad-winged butterflies. Soft and fluting came the sound of bird song. Dressed in just tee-shirts and shorts, we stepped hand in hand down the steep bank, through the twigs and feathered fern, to where the sound of running water came.

I have a photograph of Davy leaning on the wooden bridge rail, looking down the stream to where the water ran clear and sparkling over the dark broken rocks. Davy's face is half in shadow, softening the line of his jaw. His gaze, lost in the near distance, gives him an uncharacteristic thoughtfulness; almost as if on the verge of a dream, he is listening for a call.

In the field in front of us two dark horses were grazing. Davy hesitated on the raised plank of the step-up step-down wooden stile.

"I'm not sure I fancy that." He glanced at me self-consciously.

"You're not afraid of horses..."

He shrugged, shyly.

"When I was a boy, someone I knew was bitten nastily."

"I doubt if either of these are the same horse."

Davy gave me a quick look.

"You're laughing at me."

I reached up and rested a hand on his arm.

"I'll go first if you like."

Davy stepped down awkwardly.

"After you," he said.

As we began to walk across the field, Davy on my far side, the two horses raised their heads from the grass and immediately began taking long loping strides towards us. Sensing Davy tense beside me, I took his hand.

"We mustn't run, love." Squeezing his fingers, I tried to be reassuring. "They only think we've got food for them."

Davy gave me a quick glance, and looked down at his feet. Taking a breath, he quickened his stride as one of the horses nuzzled my back with its broad white nose. After a minute the most inquisitive horse, realising we were empty-handed, gave a disappointed shake of its dark mane and turned away, taking a few haughty strides before lowering its head to the grass.

When we reached the wooden gate on the other side of the field, Davy wiped his brow with the back of his hand.

"I read once that fright can take days off your life." He forced a grin, and I reached out and touched the side of his face. It's strange how the seemingly smaller moments can bring two people closer.

For a long while I wandered round the neatly kept churchyard reading the carved inscriptions on the weathered gravestones.

For
My beloved Emily
cherished wife of John Fairhurst
1806 – 1881

"They were a healthy lot down here," I called out. "Even the Victorians lived to their seventies."

Davy came back from the path and stood beside me, hesitating before he put his hands in his pockets as if we couldn't touch within the shadow of the church.

"It's the fresh country air," he said. "Kept out of the mines and the factories."

"I expect these country villages missed out on the fever and disease of the city slums."

Davy shrugged.

"Most likely, only those with money were buried here," he said. "Having money, maybe not working, they led longer lives and could afford proper gravestones. Even in a small village like this more must have died than rest in this yard."

He was probably right. How many men, women and children had lived and died here in this village over the centuries? How many were remembered? The biggest stone monument, a square sided tower with a decorative turret, was inscribed with the names of those in the village who had died overseas in the 1914 -1918 war

Many of the gravestones here were dated with the births and deaths of earlier centuries. What fascinated me was the sense of a history peopled with individuals who'd stood as I did then, with their own share of hopes and fears. But whatever had happened in their lives – whether chances had been taken or compromises made – it had still ended in exactly the same way. Each had been brought in long wooden boxes to their final resting place, absurdly beneath my feet.

Davy watched me closely, uncertain at my interest in the churchyard. He shifted from foot to foot uneasily as the sky that had been so clear all week began to cloud, obscuring the sun.

"Are you going to look inside the church?"

He sounded as if he hoped my answer would be no. Since his childhood when he'd been forced to attend Chapel, churches had given him the creeps. I smiled faintly across at him.

"I won't be long."

Leaving the gravestones, I walked up the winding cobbled pathway, past the huge stone cross that guarded the entrance to the grey stone church. The stained glass windows, reverent in a time of doubt, were protected from vandalism by a framework of thin metal bars.

Inside the church, almost instinctively I looked up. The high, arched ceiling was white-washed and divided by huge curving wooden beams which reminded me of the dark ribs of a ship-skeleton turned upside down. From the round grey stone pillars hung richly coloured pennants embroidered with heraldic coats of arms. Hanging from the ceiling on thin chains were wide crowns of dark metal which had once supported candles, but now, by some ingenious wiring, held incongruous glass light-bulbs. The red-brown wooden pews were roughly hewn and seemed too small and narrow for the people who must have come there to pray.

Was God here?

Was there a God which could accept me as I was; a man who sought another man's love? A man who expressed his true nature by this love.

Suspended in the silence, as if searching for something, I raised my head again. Where was understanding? Where was compassion? Did they lie within these stone walls, awaiting a new age? I waited for a sense of peace, but none came. I wished I could believe.

In North Cornwall, I discovered Davy had a good head for heights. Walking together along the grassy coastal downs, my stomach swam as I watched him take light steps along the cliff edge, even leaning back precariously in the buffeting wind. I think he enjoyed frightening me with his daring; it made up for the time when he'd been nervous of the horses.

On the steep rocks on the beaches, he scrambled and climbed; a forty year old boy. Reaching a jagged stone peak, he stood up, one arm outstretched, pointing out to the sea and the rugged breakers that swept in, driven by the fierce

Atlantic wind. Grey cresting white, they thundered on the shore, wave after wave.

At Studland Point a dark ridged arm of rock reached down the shingled beach, forming a natural breakwater. Clumsily I followed Davy, scrambling along its crooked length, negotiating as best I could the narrow ledges treacherously carpeted with green and brown seaweed. We paused to stare in clear rockpools, looking for the crabs and small darting fish which had been stranded by the outgoing tide. Davy gave me a curiously pink shell which I have still.

At the end of the arm of rock, sticking out of the sand, obscured and uncovered by the swell of the sea, we discovered a rusted metal cross.

Later, browsing round the cluttered Gift Shop in the small town, we found a picture of the cross in an illustrated guide to local history. I forget its name now, but it marked the line along the shore where the tide turned.

"So no one's buried there after all."

I remember Davy smiling. Since we'd discovered the cross, he'd been teasing me about the ghost that forever restless, rose from the waves, its tormented cry drowned in the roar of the sea.

Stranger even than dismantling the tent for the last time and packing our holiday gear away in the car, was our arrival back at 67 Allerton Street.

Living in college lodgings and solitary bed-sitting rooms, I'd often felt a sense of homelessness. Even when I'd been under my parents' roof, I'd never really felt I had a secure space of my own. Perhaps being homosexual increased the feeling of precariousness. Discovering myself, I'd become part of a refugee minority always uncertain of acceptance.

But that afternoon. as Davy parked the car outside our flat, I looked out at our front door and felt a strong sense of well-being; of having come *home*.

11

WE WERE sitting on the settee watching television together, when the telephone rang. Davy moved away from me to answer it.

"Oh. Justin..." He sounded surprised. "It's been ages." He smiled into the receiver. "No, well, things have been happening. I haven't been going to the pubs...I missed you too."

The words were enough to drive me out of the room.

Davy stood in the kitchen doorway while I poured tea into two mugs, apparently calm.

"Justin invited to a Halloween party."

"When?"

"Saturday."

Aware of Davy's look, I put down the teapot.

"Did you tell him about me?"

Davy shrugged. "There wasn't time. He said I could bring someone along."

There was a silence. Davy shuffled his feet uncomfortably.

"We never go anywhere these days."

It wasn't just his words, it was the sound of his voice. I tried to smile.

"We haven't needed to, have we?"

Davy didn't seem to hear me.

"It can get a bit much, lad. Staying in all the time."

"We do go out for a drink sometimes."

"I never see any of my friends."

I held my breath.

"You saw Geoff only a week ago."

Davy frowned.

"Granted. But you wanted me home before the pubs closed."

"Davy..."

The words wouldn't come. I felt as though all the air had been sucked out of the room. Davy's face flushed.

"You don't want to go the party. Do you?"

There was a pause.

"I don't mind going." Lost , I looked out of the kitchen window at our garden carpeted with autumn leaves shed from the tree next door. "Like you said, it would make a change."

Davy nodded. "You'll see, Don. A break will do us good."

Someone told me you can see what's coming in a car-crash. Everything seems to go in slow motion just before the point of impact.

On the Saturday of the party Davy came home from work with a new flattering short haircut.

Whilst the chicken curry I'd taken an hour and a half preparing dried up in the oven, he spent the longest time I could remember in the bathroom, emerging clean and sweet-smelling after his hot bath and second shave of the day. Then he took forty minutes to dress.

The party was at Justin's fourth floor council flat on a large council estate in Kentish Town. All the way there on the underground tube-train, as we rattled up the Northern line, Davy chatted to me quite relaxed as though everything was as it should be. Sad, I realised I hadn't seen him this happy, not for weeks. Not since the holiday.

I have to admit that I was hoping Justin would be ugly, but he had the natural curly brown hair which everyone else has to have to permed. Brown eyed and small-nosed, his was the pretty face of a television actor, although in fact he sold menswear in an upmarket department store.

When we arrived, he left the laughing group he'd been centre of and stepped quickly across the room to give Davy a long, welcoming kiss.

I forced a smile when I was introduced. Justin shook my hand and let it fall.

"Let's see about a drink," he said, smiling.

Linking arms with Davy, he guided him towards the crowded kitchen, to the bottles and paper cups set on a small square table. Excluded, I took a slow look round the dimly-lit room at the other party guests, some of whom were wearing improvised Halloween costumes.

Before my gaze had wandered very far, a short bearded man in blue dungarees appeared in front of me, proffering a clear plastic bowl and asking, as he looked deep into my eyes, if I wanted a crisp.

The bearded man's name was Mark and he was a lighting man for a theatre in the West End. In his mid-thirties, he assured me he'd once played Jesus in a rep production of *Godspell* in Bolton. But despite his brown beard, something in his manner made me doubt this was true. In a gesture towards Fancy Dress, Mark had put his hands into two huge silver manacles, connected by a six foot chain which dragged along the floor behind him as he returned from the kitchen with another cup of wine for me. As he tried again to look intensely into my eyes, Davy and Justin reappeared in the living room with small bottles of lager. Justin had his free arm around Davy's shoulders and, whilst they talked, he seemd to be slowly drawing Davy closer until their faces, turned to one another, were only inches apart.

The doorbell rang again and the latest guest appeared; this time a young man regaled in a skimpy black leather dress, high-heels, black stockings and a wide-brimmed witch's hat. Registering welcome with a broad smile, Justin disengaged himself from Davy with a few words and moved forward to greet this new arrival. From my corner, I watched Davy drain his bottle of lager, and glance around the room, carefully avoiding my gaze.

Perhaps I should have tried to stop what was happening, or maybe it was already too late. Perhaps what was unfolding now had begun weeks, even months ago. After all, Davy had never been faithful to me. Only since we'd started living together, I'd thought things had changed, that he was happy with just me. Uncertain, I saw Justin reclaim Davy and, leaning on his arm, lead him towards a new group of friends.

Mark pressed another paper cup of wine into my unsteady hand.

"Drink this, pet. It'll get you into the party spirit."

Smiling, I took the wine and stepped away from him, ducking my head to avoid a low-hanging paper-lantern. After that everything became jumbled and confused. I remember standing in a disconnected party circle of strangers, nodding in time to the broken conversation. Swallowing too much wine, my blurred attention became fixed on the shelves across from me and the round grinning pumpkin head, its features lit from within by a flickering candle.

Next to me a young man with bleached blond hair was confiding to a dark moustached man that he wasn't looking forward to December. Christmas was a season of dread for all men who liked men.

"Let's face it," he went on, "At Christmas the only place for a fairy is on top of the tree. Every year I spend weeks trying to persuade Paul not to go home. But of course he thinks it's his duty..."

Turning away, I almost bumped into Mark hovering behind me. His bearded lips parted in a hopeful smile.

"You need cheering up."

He reached out and took my hand firmly. Numb with

alcohol, I followed him down the crowded hallway into a room that was dark except for the lurid glow of a television in the far corner.

Through the blur of wine, I tried to focus on the flickering screen. It was a video without dialogue, set in a dimly-lit warehouse where four men were stacking heavy wooden crates. One of the men was black, one had a clone's cropped hair and clipped moustache and one was a blond muscleman. They kept laughing at the fourth man, the youngest and prettiest, who was struggling to stack boxes too heavy for him. Then the three taunting men became aware of a tear in the pretty young man's jeans, and it wasn't very long before they were all naked.

Pushing into a tight circle, the young man was held down by the black guy and the muscleman. Standing over him, the clone with the neat moustache was grinning as the pretty boy struggled, or pretended to struggle, trying to fight him off.

Looking away, I was aware of Mark reappearing beside me, pressing another paper cup of wine into my hand. Taking a swallow, my attention drifted back to the flickering screen.

"It's the black man's turn now," Mark whispered. "Look, Don, have you ever seen anything so *big?*"

Turning away from the screen, I surfaced suddenly as if out of a bad dream. I wondered what on earth I was doing here. It was a moment when everything seemed ugly. As though whatever I did, wherever I went, whoever I met, there was only ever darkness behind everything.

Then I was aware of Mark's chained hands interfering with the button-fly of my jeans. Pulling away from him, I found the door in the gloom and staggered out into the hallway.

Uncertain just where the bathroom was, I stepped over the legs of a threesome sitting on the floor of the hall passing a joint around. Fumbling with another door off the hallway, I stumbled into the bathroom. Blinking in the bright light, I twisted round, my veering reflection pursuing my gaze, mocking me from the wide pink-tinted mirrors screwed onto every wall.

Taking a deep breath, I stood over the pale peach handbasin and turned the cold tap on full. Leaning forward, I splashed cold water over my face. Still everything was spinning.

Straightening, wet-faced, I turned round for a towel, only to catch sight of a stone statuette squat on the side of the bath. A stocky man sucking his own grossly enlarged cock.

Drying myself on the faintly scented towel, I took another deep breath. Stepping back out into the dimly-lit hallway, I was aware again of the beat of music, the empty chatter and the strained laughter. I caught sight of a busy couple pressed against the far wall. It was Davy, his back to me, his attention taken up by Justin, whose hands kneaded Davy's shoulders, working in rapid time to the rhythm of Davy's kiss.

The distance which estranges lovers can settle like a frost overnight, which, instead of melting, only hardens in the light of day. No words need be said to express this: it's the way your voices change. The warmth goes from the simple words – a goodbye down the hallway as he leaves for work. Suddenly there is an emptiness and the words echo, a sadness resonant, because yesterday things were different.

Two days after the party, Davy still hadn't forgiven me. "You forced me to leave too," he'd muttered on the tense bus-ride home, taking away the hand I tried to hold.

"Davy, I saw the two of you in the hall."

"Justin's just a friend..."

And so it went on...the odd lines of argument breaking the awkward quiet.

Bewildered, I wondered how it had all happened. I wanted to say that whatever had caused the hurt and the argument didn't matter. After all, I reasoned with myself, Davy and I were still together. So I endeavoured to soak up the cold silences, hoping that if I carried on with the routine the two of us had made, our relationship, supported by habit, would somehow carry on.

The Friday after the party I stopped in at the local off-licence on my way home from work and bought four bottles of lager. It was my turn to make the dinner and I was going to prepare a vegetarian lasagne. We sometimes had a glass of wine with the evening meal, depending on the state of our finances. But lately Davy had preferred a glass of cool lager and the bottles of Red Stripe I'd purchased were his favourite brand.

As soon as I was indoors, I switched on the television news and changed hurridly out of my work shirt into a jumper and jeans. Usually I had just enough time to hang my work clothes in my wardrobe and make a pot of tea before Davy arrived home.

After he'd hung up his coat in the hall, he'd sit on the settee watching the television news while I brought in two mugs of tea on a tray and sat beside him. He was always quiet for those first minutes home, intent on Sue Lawley or Nicholas Witchell going over the headlines of the day. But between sips of tea he would, without looking at me, take my hand. Then everything was all right. It was like those moments in the night when I would wake and find him sleeping with his arms around me.

The national news ended and was replaced by a regional news summary. The tea was stewed in the pot, but still Davy hadn't come home.

I wondered if he was working late. Maybe he was having a drink with his work mates. Usually he rang and let me know because dinner would be late. The minutes passed slowly, but there was no phone call. No sound of his key turning in the front door. I remembered a giant poster I'd seen on the underground walls informing the public how every minute someone in the United Kingdom was involved in a motor accident. Even pedestrians were at risk...

I told myself I was being silly. There had to be a perfectly ordinary reason why he was late. I made myself go into the kitchen and start preparing the meal; slicing the onions and aubergines and putting them into a frying pan, chopping up the garlic and adding the tomatoes.

Just after half past eight the lasagne was cooked through and ready to eat. Still he wasn't home.

Piling my plate, I sat on my own at the small round kitchen table and forced myself to eat. I only remembered the lager cooling in the refrigerator when the meal was three-quarters finished. It seemed like a joke now; buying the lager as a surprise for someone who wasn't there.

Where was he?

Crouched on the settee, I watched the Nine O'Clock News. Jan Leeming, her face troubled, spoke of the latest murder in Northern Ireland; then, less concerned, spoke of the local authorities' rebellion against rate-capping. Last of all there was the weather forecaster, an eccentric jumpy man with glasses, who promised a little November sunshine.

Turning off the television, I began to cry. I knew where Davy was. Knew as surely as if I could see the two of them, him and Justin, in bed together.

Packing my shirts and socks into a leather holdall, I told myself I had never wanted love. All love had ever done was twist me. I put in my pants and handkerchiefs, telling myself how it was loving someone that had made me insecure...

Then I unpacked the bag, put my shirts and socks, my pants and handkerchiefs back into the chest of drawers. It was as though I was going mad.

Just after midnight the telephone rang.

"Is that you, Don?" It was Davy's voice. But changed, uncertain.

"Davy, where are you?"

"A phone box."

I held my breath.

"I'm in a mess, boy." His voice wavered.

I wanted him to keep silent, so afraid I was of what he would say.

"Just come home, Davy."

There was a long pause. The muscles in my stomach tightened as though under a stranger's hand. I could sense Davy taking a deep breath.

"I saw Justin tonight."

Closing my eyes, I felt my hands begin to shake.

"I *saw* Justin." His voice broke.

"Davy...let's not talk. Not now. Just come home. Please."

There was a click and the line went dead.

I pretended to be asleep when he climbed into bed beside me. For a long time he was completely still in the darkness. Without even turning to look, some sixth sense told me he was lying on his back, staring up at the ceiling. Afraid to speak, I waited, wondering if he knew I was still awake.

It must have been nearly an hour before he shifted towards me and held me in his arms without a word.

After that everything was awful. I felt as though I'd stepped into a nightmare. But it wasn't a dream. It wasn't just a fever born of jealousy. It was real, it had happened. That evening Davy had gone to bed with Justin. He'd held and kissed and come with him.

I was silent at first. Davy stepped round me carefully like someone afraid. And when at last he touched me, I started crying and couldn't stop. Uncertain, he held me until my tears subsided. But even as he embraced me, even as he rocked me in his arms, I couldn't escape the feeling that something was over between us.

With his betrayal with Justin, something had died in me. I felt as if a line had been crossed. Even if I wanted to, I couldn't have gone back.

As he stroked my forehead and gently kissed away my tears, I cried because of his tenderness, because I loved him, because nothing between us would ever be the same again. The private world our love had made was destroyed and lost forever now. Not that any of this was said. Davy continued to hold me until, exhausted, I slept, my blotched face pressed into the pillow, still cradled in his arms.

Coming back from the West End one afternoon, I was walking along the platform of the underground tube station, glancing at the posters spread on the billboards along the tunnel as I waited for my train. Quite unexpectedly, as if I'd been lightly touched on the shoulder, something made me stop, turn my head and look across at the people clustered together on the opposite platform, awaiting the eastbound train.

Someone seemed familiar to me. Focusing intuitively on the short, stocky figure in jeans and a padded jacket, I thought I recognised the stance, the short spiky black hair. If only I could see his face...

In that moment there was a mechanical rumble, the rushing sound of air as the eastbound train drew in, obscuring everyone.

When I reached our flat in Allerton Street, I was aware of the acrid smell of burning. Stepping back into the road, I saw black smoke rising over the roof, a dark plume climbing against a grey sky.

It was Davy's work.

He stood in the back garden completely oblivious of me.

Hunched in an anorak, he tended the bonfire he'd made on the bare bed where in the summer the scented stocks and the lavender had been. Now, amongst the roaring orange flames I recognised the pattern of the old living-room curtains, saw dim faces dissolve in a curl of blistering photographs. An arm of a discarded shirt shivered as it caught fire. Working busily with a shovel, Davy sweated as he painstakingly rebuilt the blaze, making sure everything he'd thrown out, every part of a past, was consumed.

Watching him work, absorbed amongst the fire and ashes, my heart twisted. Love doesn't die all at once, but slowly, piece by piece. The fire crackled and spat. A wintry breeze dragged the black smoke higher still over the roofs.

Suddenly aware of my presence, Davy turned in the fading afternoon light and smiled at me, his face lit with flame.

12

HE WAS sitting in our usual corner in the cafe, a copy of the *Guardian* folded in half on the table in front of him. Reading intently, he flicked his cigarette ash blindly into the nearest green glass ashtray, reached automatically for his coffee.

"You still come here, then."

He looked up, the blue eyes unable to help their surprise. "Hello."

I could almost feel us both tremble. He stubbed the cigarette out, ground it round in the ashtray, giving himself time to think. Uncertain, I rested my hands on the back of the chair opposite him, and waited.

I'd met Jimmy on an underground tube-train coming home from work one evening. Formerly an engineer for British Telecom, he was twenty-four now and studying Sociology and Politics at London University. Three inches shorter than I was, strong but compactly built, he had black hair long enough to look soft, short enough to look spiky. Blue-eyed, an apparently permanent two-day growth of beard gave him a refugee-look. Often two people know each other is homosexual; it's understood in a glance. It was like that with Jimmy and me.

Slightly pale-faced, Jimmy's darting glance gave a misleading impression of shyness. He smoked cigarettes feverishly. I told him he should stop to protect his health and he laughed; he had a gritty laugh at odds with his face.

Everything, he said, was bad for you. Nicotine. Coffee. Salt.

Sex...He called AIDS Arse Injected Death, but had a friend who was dying from it in a Paddington hospital. Despite his teasing, it frightened him. I'd never realised the extent of the tragedy. Over a hundred and fifty people in Britain had died then. Jimmy called it the new epidemic.

Brought together by chance, we fell into a habit of meeting twice a week at five thirty on Hammersmith tube station. Occasionally we had a quick coffee in a small grubby cafe off the Broadway. I never explained anything or said a word about Davy, but Jimmy joked about my always having to hurry home.

One evening, after we'd finished the coffee, Jimmy fidgeted with the empty cups as if afraid to look at me. In the awkward silence I kept glancing at my wristwatch, nervous of the time. Just as I stood up to leave, Jimmy said he wanted us to make love. Hearing the hushed words, I realised I wanted him too.

If only it could have been as simple as that. But Davy had taught me just how complicated this business of feeling could be. Suddenly I was scared.

For a week I stopped taking the tube-train home. Stopped waiting for him at Hammersmith Broadway. Although it was a longer, less comfortable route, I began taking the bus instead, pushing in the crowd for a seat. Stupidly, I used to catch myself glancing out of the grimy bus window, hoping to see somewhere in the milling crowds, Jimmy's face...

And then I went back.

Jimmy rolled up his copy of the *Guardian* and put the newspaper in his grey canvas shoulder-bag together with his cigarettes and college books.

"Can I get you a coffee, Don?"

He made his voice light, but I thought I could read a hesitancy in his mouth.

For a few long moments we both wondered what would happen next. Taking a breath, I repeated the words over in my head, at last heard my voice curiously steady despite my doubt.

"Is there somewhere we can go?"

Jimmy lived in a dim bed-sit on the third floor of a tall neglected house fifteen minutes walk from Hammersmith Broadway. It was the sort of room where you keep the electric light turned on during the day because so little daylight creeps in through the small square window. In the late November afternoon it was already chill, reminding me of my damp room in Chelsea.

Like most bed-sits there was only the most basic furniture: a three-quarter bed, a battered wardrobe and a chest of drawers. In a narrow alcove there was a stained sink, an antique cooker and a cupboard whose doors didn't properly shut. The refrigerator, shared with another tenant, hummed outside on the landing.

What I couldn't get over was the mess the room was in. The lone table was covered with books, screwed-up envelopes, biscuit-wrappers, antiperspirant, postcards, apples and an orange and a half-full bottle of red wine with three dirty glasses. Clothes, jeans, tee-shirts, socks and jumpers littered the floor. The duvet lay twisted on the bed.

"I tidy on Sundays," Jimmy said, unperturbed. "You came at the wrong end of the week."

Glancing round for somewhere to sit. I saw the solitary hard-backed chair was occupied by a pile of books: novels, sociological and political texts. It seemed too much of an invitation if I sat on the bed. Shy of movement, I stood where I was, searching for the right thing to say. Jimmy came closer to me and took my hand, gently stroking my palm, reminding me of Davy. Thinking of him, I tried to resist the impulse to pull away.

"I can't stay long."

Jimmy laughed, let my hand go.

"You're a real Greta Garbo."

"Sorry." I flushed, embarrassed.

"I want to be alone." Jimmy put on a pretend Scandinavian voice, then smiled. "It makes you very mysterious, always rushing off."

"Is that the only reason you like me?"

I suppose I sounded hurt. Jimmy gave me a quiet look, his expression changing completely, making him suddenly seem older. "Hold on now. You're being over-sensitive."

"I'm just nervous."

Walking to the small window, I looked out onto a dismal prospect of disrepaired and neglected houses, littered back yards. Sensibly, Jimmy stayed where he was, half-leaning against the table.

"Why are you so uncomfortable, Don?"

"I live with someone."

In the silence that followed, Jimmy came over to me and gently rested his hands on my shoulders.

"I guessed that," he whispered. "But you're here."

"I know."

"It won't hurt you to kiss me."

Again I stepped away, ducking my head, confused by my desire and the disquieting sense of betrayal which hovered like a ghost. Because I wanted to hold Jimmy, I couldn't look at him.

"I've only had one lover."

Jimmy sat down on the bed, tugged at the roll collar of his black polo-neck sweater. He searched round for his cigarettes, fussed with a match.

" This lover," he said. "I suppose he's the someone you live with."

"Yes..."

Jimmy exhaled blue smoke, half-smiled.

"I'm tempted to say it doesn't matter," he said, looking at me carefully. "But I can see it does to you."

There was a silence. Jimmy waited for me to glance at him,

then he smiled, trying to reassure me.

"Anyway, I'm glad you came to the cafe today." He smiled again. "I'd given you until the end of the week, so you made it just in time."

Not knowing how to respond, I noticed on the crowded table the cover of an Alison Lurie novel I'd read and enjoyed. Perhaps we could talk about this? At the same time I glanced at my watch. Already I would be late. Davy would be waiting for me at home. It was his turn to cook tonight. Still wondering how I could leave now, whether I should stay, I watched Jimmy remove the pile of books from the chair and put them on the cluttered table.

"Sit yourself down." He gave me a quick look. "I'll put the kettle on for coffee."

We kissed once before we said goodbye. I'd felt myself tremble. On impulse as we stood on the front doorstep he rushed back upstairs, returning with a Christopher Isherwood novel which he put into my hands without a word, as though that alone would guarantee my return.

His last smile was happy, confident.

"We'll forget the coffee-bar," he said, turning to face me. "You know where I live now."

When I arrived home Davy was curled up on the settee watching snooker on television – Hurricane Higgins versus his favourite and fellow Welshman, Terry Griffiths.

"Where have you been, boy? I was getting worried."

"Sorry, Davy...I should have rung."

Backing out of the living room into the hall, I hung up my coat, hesitating, wondering whether I should shelter for a moment in the kitchen. Davy's voice made me start.

"What kept you?" He called out over the background hum of television commentary.

I hesitated.

"Kerry needed to talk. Boyfriend trouble. She dragged me into a West End pub to tell me all about it. The phone there was out of order..."

Appalled, I stopped. Leaning forward, I pressed my face into the folds of my hanging overcoat. It was the first time I'd ever lied to him.

"She needed to talk, then," Davy called.

"Yes..." My voice seemed to echo. Tears pricked the back of my eyes. It hurt more because it was so easy to lie to him. Because he trusted me.

Few of us in this world are brave. When a shadow falls across the future, our instinct is not to step forward, but to turn back in an effort to recapture the past, as if by this escape the present will stand still.

At Richmond Davy and I walked along besides the broad grey river, hunch-shouldered against the chill wind which carried and cast the dying leaves out onto the water. In the summer we'd had a cheese and pickle picnic here and been barely able to find a free space on the grass littered with sunbathers and tourists in tee-shirts and sunglasses. Now, not a soul idled on the green, and only a few people muffled in thick coats and scarves followed our waterside path until the river turned in a great bend, disappearing in a wide glimmering curve behind the trees.

We began then to climb the steep bank, finding a winding path under the reaching branches. Quietly, Davy sang to me as we reached the wide road.

"What's it called?" I took his hand for a moment.

He smiled self-consciously.

"*Autumn Leaves*."

I laughed.

"Who sang it originally? Sinatra?"

"Nat King Cole."

"Never heard of him."

Davy cuffed my hair with a gentle fist.

"The ignorance of the younger generation."

He looked into my eyes. We might have kissed then, but for a middle-aged couple coming towards us, the wife holding the lead of their dog, one of those curly black poodles with the built-in frantic yap.

The entrance to the wood was a wide yellowstone archway over an elaborate black iron gate. We walked off the gravel path under the arch, through the long pale grass beneath the trees, their dark branches stuck with the last brown and red leaf-stars like a child's picture.

Davy touched my arm to stop me as we came across a small group of deer. Dark-coated and nervous-eyed, they dipped their heads to nibble the grass, never completely still on their delicate legs. At that moment, the afternoon sun freed itself at last from the ragged clouds and cast a brilliant light down over the wood, turning the late autumn colours to gold.

After we made love, we lay still together. Davy stroked my face with his fingertips.

"Beautiful," he whispered.

He moved to hold me closer in his arms, a curious beseech in his embrace as if he knew everything. He murmured my name as if to call me back. Watching my face, he traced the curve of my lips with his fingers. But I could not speak.

The Christmas season was in full swing. Christmas trees and tinsel glittered in the shop windows. Santa Claus was everywhere. The Salvation Army van toured the streets blaring a recorded rendition of *Once in Royal David's City*. In a London hospital the one hundred and seventieth victim died of AIDS. At work the Christmas Committee began planning the seasonal party. Two weeks before Christmas we spent a quiet afternoon in the office putting up brightly-coloured paper chains.

Retracing my way along the streets from Hammersmith Broadway, I worried that I'd left everything too late. Probably by now he'd met someone else. Maybe he'd never really wanted me...

Looking up at the four-storey house I thought how strange it was not to be able to see his window; to visit a house where there was no evidence that Jimmy even existed, no obvious space that was his. Remembering the untidiness of his room, I wondered if the disorder was his way of dealing with the precariousness of his life. Maybe he was less afraid than I?

Ringing the bell marked "Third Floor" I felt sure he wouldn't answer. Suddenly I wanted to run away. But just where could I go? Soon I would have to take responsibility for my feelings, but just now, *just now* I needed to see him. And hold him. Have him close.

Standing on the doorstep in the darkness, I pressed the doorbell again, at once wretched and full of hope. No one answered.

Maybe he was out. Maybe he'd even moved away. Students changed rooms all the time...

Scared, I rang the bell a final time, glancing along the grey littered street while I waited. The street lamps flickered on one by one, a blink of electricity. Muffled by the front door, faint at last came the sound of footsteps on the stairs.

also by Timothy Ireland:

WHO LIES INSIDE

...It was as if out of the corner of my eye I could see a stranger standing in the shadows and I was scared to look too closely in case I saw who it was. Worst of all the stranger seemed to have wriggled under my skin, or had grown inside me all my eighteen years; only now for some reason that stranger was not content to stay in the shadows but wanted to step out into the light and be seen...

This acclaimed novel won the Other Award in 1984.

"This excellent, very readable short novel is written with an immediacy and freshness which captures perfectly the confused and isolated pain of adolescence, and in particular the special angst involved in the discovery of sexuality" – *Time Out*.

"An excellent book which deals with family and adolescent relationships in sufficient depth for teachers to consider its use with their classes. This is an exciting, innovative book which deserves the widest possible readership – it will open your eyes to some issues about gay men and must be made available to young people themselves" – *ILEA Contact*.

"That rare thing, a simple, moving, clearly-written novel, truthful and affecting" – *Body Politic*.

ISBN 0 907040 30 6   £3.95

Rohase Piercy
MY DEAREST HOLMES

Although Dr Watson is known for recording nearly sixty of his adventures with the celebrated detective Sherlock Holmes, he also wrote other reminiscences of their long friendship which were never intended for publication during their lifetimes. Rescued from oblivion by Rohase Piercy, here are two previously unknown stories about the great detective and his companion, throwing a fresh light upon their famous partnership and helping to explain much which has puzzled their devotees.

"Thoroughly amusing...Wonderful stuff" – Stanley Reynolds, *Guardian*.

"Any Holmes aficianado would enjoy it for its own sake" – *Gay Times*.

"These pieces work on a number of levels – the detective story (written in a style amazingly close to the originals), and the social document. Most importantly, a literate and humane portrait of one man's love for another" – *Gay Life*.

ISBN 0 85449 081 7 £3.95

Jeremy Beadle
DEATH SCENE

The discovery of Guy Latimer's mutilated body in an alleyway near one of London's leading gay nightclubs opens this intriguing and compulsive novel. It soon becomes apparent that the killing was premeditated and that the assailant must have been known to the victim. Suspicion falls on Guy's circle of gay friends, all of whom seem to be hiding crucial information, but who find themselves obliged to join forces to try and solve the killing, fearful of a set-up by the police.

A highly innovative and cleverly plotted mystery that in classic whodunnit style grips the reader until the very last pages. The first of a new genre – a contemporary gay murder story set in present-day Britain, with sharp observations on both the nature of the gay community in post-AIDS London and on the reactions and attitudes of the wider community around it.

ISBN 0 85449 088 4   £4.95

A. T. Fitzroy
DESPISED AND REJECTED

This major piece of gay literary history was first published at the height of the First World War. Focusing on the brutal persecution of conscientious objectors, and with its two main characters a lesbian and a gay man, it was almost immediately banned. This is its first reissue in Britain for seventy years.

In a new introduction written for this edition Jonathan Cutbill examines the background to the novel and the trial of its original publisher.

"Fitzroy presents the socialist-pacifist cause with intelligence and passion and manages to avoid sentimentality. She entertainingly lampoons the social pretensions, patriotic double-think, snobbery, smugness and bloodlust" – Peter Parker, *Times Literary Supplement*.

"A thoughtful and well-considered book...brave and pioneering. Compelling fiction about a world that may seem light years away – but from which many attitudes still prevail" – *Gay Times*.

ISBN 0 85449 063 9   £5.95

Distributed in North America by
Alyson Publications Inc.,
40 Plympton Street, Boston, MA 02118, USA
telephone: (617) 542 5679

GMP books can be ordered from any bookshop in the UK, and from
specialised bookshops overseas. If you prefer to order by mail, please send
full retail price plus £1.50 for postage and packing to: GMP Publishers Ltd
(G.B.), PO Box 247, London N17 9QR. (for Access/Eurocard/Mastercard/
Visa/American Express, give number and signature.) Comprehensive mail-
order catalogue also available.

In North America order from Alyson Publications Inc.,
40 Plympton St, Boston MA 02118, USA.

NAME AND ADDRESS IN BLOCK LETTERS PLEASE:

Name _

Address _

_ _

_ _

_ _